"Do you hate women, Luke? All women?"

His breath hissed between his teeth. "Lay off, Sally. All I said was that I don't want an affair with *you*."

Sally flinched. All her feelings of inadequacy rushed to the surface. She wasn't sure she even wanted an affair, but to be found undesirable...

"Can you not bear the thought of making love to me?" she asked miserably. "It's important to me to know."

"Sally, go to bed. This has gone on long enough."

"You can't send me to bed like a naughty child," Sally snapped, angry now. "I'm a grown woman."

Very deliberately he unzipped his pants and stepped out of them. "That, my dear, is part of the problem."

Sally suddenly felt a twinge of something that she just didn't want to identify....

SANDRA FIELD, once a biology technician, now writes full-time under the pen names of Jocelyn Haley and Jan MacLean. She lives with her son in Canada's Maritimes, which she often uses as a setting for her books. She loves the independent life-style she has as a writer. She's her own boss, sets her own hours, and increasingly there are travel opportunities.

Books by Sandra Field

Don't miss any of our special offers. Write to us at the following address for information on our newest releases.

Harlequin Reader Service
901 Fuhrmann Blvd., P.O. Box 1397, Buffalo, NY 14240
Canadian address: P.O. Box 603,
Fort Erie, Ont. L2A 5X3

SANDRA FIELD

love in a mist

Harlequin Books

TORONTO • NEW YORK • LONDON
AMSTERDAM • PARIS • SYDNEY • HAMBURG
STOCKHOLM • ATHENS • TOKYO • MILAN

Harlequin Presents first edition November 1988
ISBN 0-373-11120-7

Original hardcover edition published in 1988
by Mills & Boon Limited

PROLOGUE

WITH a break in her voice Ms Cindy Morley said, 'You must have had a fight with your wife this morning, Mr Sheridan.'

'I don't have a wife.'

'Oh.' Cindy pouted her scarlet lips. 'You mean you've never been married?'

'Ms Morley, we're not discussing my marital status. We're discussing the file on Robert Carpenter, which seems to have vanished into the ether. I need that file. I need it for the directors' meeting, which is due to begin in exactly fifteen minutes.'

'Mrs Axworthy could find it for me.' Mrs Axworthy was the secretary for the head of the parole board.

'Then get Mrs Axworthy over here. Now.'

Cindy crossed her legs, revealing a strategic amount of silk-clad thigh. 'I don't think you like me, Mr Sheridan.'

'The Carpenter file, Ms Morley.'

Cindy reached for the phone, exposing more thigh, dialled Mrs Axworthy's extension, spoke prettily into the receiver and then said to Luke, 'She'll be right along. You know, I overheard someone in the canteen say you were divorced.'

'That's correct,' Luke said shortly.

'So am I, isn't that a coincidence? It's difficult sometimes, isn't it?' Without altering her expression in the slightest Cindy allowed her big blue eyes to widen and acquire a sheen of tears. 'You must come to my place some time so we can compare notes.' And she leaned forward, exposing an undeniably alluring cleavage, and rested her hand on his wrist. To his horrified fascination a tear gathered on her lashes.

Mrs Axworthy, stout, grimly efficient, pushed open the door. As Luke stood transfixed, no doubt the picture of guilt, Cindy brushed her breasts against his sleeve and said, 'Oh, Mrs Axworthy, I'm so glad you're here—Mr Sheridan is so cross with me. I can't seem to find the Carpenter file.'

'Check the manual, page 34-B,' said Mrs Axworthy, approaching the computer and Cindy with impartial firmness.

Five minutes later Mrs Axworthy handed Cindy a printout of the file and marched out of the office. Cindy passed Luke the sheaf of paper with a dazzling smile, as if she had accomplished something particularly clever all by herself. 'There you go!' she said. 'And you've still got five minutes before your meeting.'

Luke took the opposite corner of the file, his hand as far from the scarlet fingernails as possible. 'Thank you,' he said.

But Cindy did not release her grip on the file. She swayed towards him, enveloping him in a cloud of heavy perfume and rampant sexuality. 'Any time,' she said, pinioning him with her forget-me-not blue eyes.

Luke, who stood a foot taller than she and weighed at least seventy pounds more, fled. He hurried down the hall, forgetting his briefcase and his notes for the meeting, and banged his fist on his boss's door. Ross Deighton's gravelly voice said, 'Come in.'

Luke entered the office, pulled the door shut behind him and said pungently, 'I'll do you a straight trade, Ross—Mrs Axworthy for that blonde bombshell that those idiots in personnel have dumped on me.'

Ross leaned back in his chair. He was a short, grey-haired man nearing retirement; a lifetime of working within the prison system had not entirely quenched his sense of humour or his innate optimism. 'She's only been here for six days,' he said. 'Give her time.'

'Another six days and she'll be raping me.'

Ross gave the short bark that passed for laughter with him. 'Come on, Luke, you're a big boy, you can look after yourself.'

Luke said bitterly, 'I asked them to hire me a nice soul who knows how to file and measures forty, forty, forty. But do they do that? ''Oh no, that's discrimination on the basis of age, we can't do that, Mr Sheridan, we'd have the human rights commission down on us.'' So I get stuck with a blonde chick with a skin-tight sweater and nails the colour of blood who drapes herself all over me every chance she gets and can't spell worth a damn. Sexual harassment, that's what it is.' And Luke slammed the Carpenter file on Ross's desk.

Ross made a steeple out of his fingers and said mildly, 'You could always try taking her up on it.'

Luke scowled at him. 'No, thanks!'

'Give me one good reason why not.'

'I don't feel like hopping in the sack with the first female who comes along. Particularly if she's got red fingernails.'

'Dating anyone, Luke?'

'What is this, a counselling session?'

'Had any affairs the past year?'

'No, I have not. Not that it's any of your business.'

Even more mildly Ross said, 'Still hung up on Althea, Luke?'

'I am not hung up on Althea! The divorce was finalised over a year ago.'

'A year in which you've worked like a madman. I've been watching you, Luke—and worrying about you, if you want the truth.'

Pointedly Luke looked at his watch. 'The directors'

meeting's due to start in thirty seconds.'

Ross's answer was to speak into his intercom. 'Mrs Axworthy, delay the meeting ten minutes, will you? Thanks.' Then he looked across at the dark-haired man towering over his desk. 'Sit down, Luke, I want to talk to you.'

Reluctantly Luke sat down and crossed his legs. Although he liked Ross and respected his judgement, he was not in the mood to listen to any sermons about the women—or lack of them—in his life.

'I think you should take a week off,' Ross began. 'Some time next month. July's a great time to get away somewhere. Find yourself a cottage by the beach or a cabin in the woods and vegetate for a week. Do you a world of good, and I'll be willing to bet the parole board won't fall apart without you, valuable though your services are.' Thoughtfully Ross considered his linked fingers. 'You might even take a woman with you. To the cottage, I mean.'

'I'm doing very well without a woman,' Luke said tightly.

'Yeah? You're single again, Luke—you're not married any more. You seem to be forgetting that. No reason you shouldn't have your holiday with a woman. There *are* some without red fingernails, and a good affair never hurt anyone.'

In a clipped voice Luke said, 'An affair is the last thing I need.' He ran his fingers around his collar, making a visible effort to relax. 'You know that I'm taking a leave of absence in September to teach at St Mary's and to do some research in Halifax. I hardly need a vacation in July as well.'

'When a blonde chick, as you call her, can get you this riled up, then I think you do need a vacation.' Ross leaned forward, his face very serious. 'Come on, Luke, we both know the stress-factor in your job. I've told you often enough you're the best man in the system in

eastern Canada—which means you get a lion's share of
the problem cases. You're in and out of the pen every
day, you're dealing with hardened criminals some of
whom would stick a knife in you as soon as talk to you,
you were involved in the hostage-taking in February
and you regularly get threats from inmates who've
been released but who don't think you got them
paroled soon enough.'

'I can handle all that.'

'Yes, I expect you can . . . but you're not invincible,
Luke. The reason you're the best man I've got is that
you care—you get involved, you've got guts, you can
somehow run the tightrope between toughness and
compassion and end up with an inmate's respect. We
both know that's not easy. And we both know it costs.'

'I enjoy my job,' Luke said shortly.

'Sure you do. But you haven't taken a holiday since
the divorce and I wouldn't want to count how much
overtime you've put in during the last year. You're
running a very real danger of burnout. Draw on your
inner reserves for too long, and you'll find one day that
you don't have any left. And that's when you start
getting as hardened as some of the guys you deal with.
I don't want to see that happen to you.'

Luke raked his fingers through his hair, his sea-blue
eyes perplexed. He, more than Ross, knew how
desperately he had thrown himself into work the last
year, and while he might not appreciate Ross's
directness he had the fairness to admit there was truth
in his assessment. He allowed his mind to picture a
cottage by the beach, the rhythmic sigh of surf, the
gleam of sand, and felt his spirits quicken. Maybe Ross
was right. Maybe he did need a holiday. And at least it
would get him, if only temporarily, out of the clutches
of Ms Cindy Morley.

Ross was a shrewd judge of character. 'Good,' he
said briskly. 'Fill out the leave form whenever you've

made your plans, and I'll see there aren't any hitches.'
He stood up. 'Now, we'd better go in there and face the
music. The two new members they've appointed are
bleeding hearts of the worst kind. They want Matt
Coolihan released, can you believe it?'

Matt Coolihan had murdered three people outside
prison and one inside; Luke, who was six feet two,
weighed one hundred and eighty pounds and was an
expert in self-defence, never interviewed Matt alone.
'Might as well release Jack the Ripper,' he said equably,
stretching to his full height and feeling happier than he
had in weeks. He added soberly, 'Thanks, Ross—if I'm
a half-decent parole officer, you've got to be the best
boss I could possibly have. I'll take that holiday. 'I've
been thinking about it while we were talking—a couple
of friends of mine went to those little French islands off
the coast of Newfoundland last summer. St Pierre and
Miquelon. They had a great time. If I'm not too late to
get bookings, I might go there. Brush up on my French,
drink a bit of wine, do some deep-sea fishing.'

Ross knew better than to mention the word affair
again. 'Make sure you enjoy yourself,' he said.

Luke grinned. 'I reckon I will, Ross. Yeah, I reckon I
will.'

CHAPTER ONE

LYNETTE said forcefully, Do you know what you need, Sally? You need a damn good affair!'

As Sally grimaced at her friend, the sunlight gleamed in her short copper curls. 'Now if you'd said I needed a new washing machine or a thirty-six-hour day or a resident housekeeper I'd have agreed. But an affair? The last thing I need is an affair, Lyn.'

'You're quite wrong, you know.' The sea breeze stirred the thin pleated cotton of Lynette's shirt. She affected a somewhat Bohemian style of dress, and because she was small and blue-eyed and artistic, she might have been thought of as helpless. Sally knew better. Lynette had strong opinions on almost any subject one could think of, and was not backward in expressing those opinions. Yet she could be both sensitive and tactful and was always warm-hearted, and for these reasons Sally usually paid attention to her pronouncements.

So now Sally said agreeably, 'Tell me all the reasons I'm wrong—have you got them listed? Alphabetically?'

Lynette laughed. 'You know me too well.'

'We've been friends for four years . . . since Cecilia was born.'

'And Bruce left,' Lynette said crisply.

'Yes.' A shadow crossed Sally's eyes, which were the colour of the ocean on a misty day. 'It all seems so long ago, as if it happened to another person.'

'Well, it didn't. It happened to you. You're a beautiful woman who's scared to death of men because you've made a prison cell out of your memories.'

Sally sighed and lay back on the grassy bank, clasping her hands behind her head and closing her eyes. Had she been asked she would have described herself as ordinary rather than beautiful; average height, a normal figure, regular features. What she would have missed were the contradicitons: the astonishingly vibrant colour of her hair coupled with the wariness in her grey-green eyes; the strength in her chin and the vulnerability in the soft curve of her lips; the unstudied grace of her movements that in no way detracted from her air of remoteness, of being in some very real way unapproachable.

She said lazily, not opening her eyes, 'Past history, Lynette. We don't have to talk about it now. I finished the final printout of a Master's thesis yesterday and it's a gorgeous day in June, let's enjoy the sun.'

A gull drifted from the sky to land on the cove, ripples spreading outwards on the smooth water, the bird's plumage whiter than the foam that splashed on the rocks at the mouth of the cove. Lynette said craftily, 'Do you ever think of remarrying?'

'Oh, I suppose so. Some day.'

'Some day! Today, tomorrow, some day, never. Be honest, Sally—you mean never.'

Lynette was not going to give up. 'You're being very vehement,' Sally said. 'What's up?'

'I'm worried about you.'

'I'm fine, Lyn. The word processor's nearly paid for, Caleb did well in school, and Cecilia is a darling. What more do I need?'

'A man.'

Sally sat up and said irritably, 'You're pushing your luck, Lynette—let's drop this conversation.

'When I first met you I could understand why you kept your distance from the male of the species; you'd had a rough deal and a whole load of responsibilities dumped on you and I'm sure a man *was* the last thing you needed. But then Dennis moved in down the road and the two of you started dating, and even if Dennis wasn't the type I would have picked for you, I figured it was a start. That was two years ago, and I've been biting my tongue ever since. Dennis is as much in love with you as he's capable of being in love with anyone and he'd marry you tomorrow, but are you engaged to him? No, ma'am. You're playing it safe by dating a man who is, to put it politely, non-assertive, and who has about as much sex appeal as a dead codfish. When are you going to smarten up, Sally? I'm sure Dennis is a very nice man—but you deserve better than him.'

'I've been married once. I'm in no hurry to be married again.'

'So you're going to live like a nun for the next ten years?'

Sally managed a smile. 'Most nuns don't have four-year-old daughters.'

'I know how much you love Cecilia. But at the age of twenty-two you shouldn't be revolving your life around your daughter. You know what your problem is? You're all hung up on sex. Your idea of a relationship is a meeting of minds: pure, ethereal and safe. Nothing as vulgar as getting into bed with someone.'

'I don't *want* to get in bed with anyone!'

'At least you're admitting it.'

Sally's cheeks were pink with temper. 'All right, so I've got a hang-up about sex. When I was seventeen I made love with Bruce in the back seat of his father's car, and, innocents that we were, I ended up pregnant. Bruce was forced into marrying me, he ran away eight months later and divorced me a year ago. I was left holding the baby, and with a guilt-complex as big as—as a container ship. And no, I did not enjoy sex with Bruce. I hated it, if you want the truth. And since I don't believe in making the same mistake twice, I've avoided sexual involvement ever since.' She glared at her friend. 'Now are you happy?'

Lynette said thoughtfully, 'It would be best if you could get away somewhere. Go on a holiday, meet some hunk of a man and have a nice healthy affair. Get rid of all your inhibitions, then come home and find someone to marry. That's the way to do it—this place is too small for you to have an affair here. For one thing, everyone in the cove would know what you were up to. But more importantly I think you should make love with someone you know you'll never meet again. You'd have so much more freedom that way.'

'Well, you can forget that idea,' Sally said more easily. 'I can't afford to go away.'

By Sally's standards Lynette was rich; but she had never damaged Sally's pride by offering to help her financially. 'You couldn't afford it even after you get paid for the thesis?'

'No. A new washing machine is a much greater priority.'

'A rich husband would solve so many of your problems. He could pay for the washing machine and Caleb's education and a whole new wardrobe for you.'

'I expect if he was rich he'd have his own washing machine. Lyn, I'm sure it would be all very wonderful if I could get away on holiday and meet some knight in shining armour——'

'I don't want him to be too chivalrous—I want him to seduce you!'

'But it isn't going to happen. So let's forget it, huh?'

'If a holiday could be arranged in some way that you could afford, would you go?'

Sally was perfectly sure it couldn't be arranged. 'Sure,' she said.

'Promise?'

'Promise . . . although who'd want to leave here in

the summer?'

Here was Stellars Cove, an inlet of the Atlantic not far
from the entrance to Halifax Harbour in Nova Scotia.
The cove was long and narrow, edged with fishing
shacks on stilts and a higgledy-piggledy array of houses
that ranged from summer cottages to the expensive
new cedar homes of city doctors and lawyers. Yachts
and Cape Islanders democratically circled their
moorings on the slow rise and fall of the tides; the
fragrance of old-fashioned climbing roses mingled with
the sharper scents of seaweed and diesel fuel and fish.

Sally lived in the clapboard house that had belonged
to her father and mother; the lawn sloped to the rocks
on the shoreline. Since her mother's death three years
ago she had planted annuals and perennials in untidy
profusion all around the house and thrown away the
Venetian blinds that had shaded the windows for as
long as she could remember. She had often wished she
could as easily throw off her mother's strict moral
precepts and forget the anger that had eaten away at
her mother's soul. Her mother had never forgiven Sally
for getting pregnant at the age of seventeen.

The screen door squeaked behind them and Cecilia
came out on the porch clutching her rag doll; she had
fallen asleep on the chesterfield after lunch. There could
never be any question whose daughter she was, for she
had a tangle of red-gold curls, a temperament to match,
and wide-spaced eyes the same chameleon-like shade
between grey and green as Sally's. 'I'm thirsty,' she
said.

'I made lemonade this morning, I'll bring some out,'
Sally offered. 'Why don't you come and sit with
Lynette?'

Cecilia liked Lynette, who sometimes brought her old
tubes of paint and brushes to play with. She padded
across the grass in her bare feet and curled up against
Lynette. 'Where's Caleb?' she asked. Caleb Dexter was

Sally's brother.

'Your mother said he'd gone to Cranberry Head to look for a job.' Lynette lived at Cranberry Head, a peninsula projecting into the ocean south of the cove, and peopled by a motley collection of artists, writers and musicians, some of whom had considerable talent, others of whom had talent only for a self-consciously artistic life-style. Lynette fell somewhere in between.

As Sally came back on the porch, balancing a tray of glasses, the front gate banged shut and her brother shouted, 'Where are you, Sal?'

'Round the back,' she called, passing Lynette and Cecilia their glasses.

Caleb was not alone. He was hauled round the corner of the house by a very large dog who was pulling so hard on its rope that its breath was being emitted in hoarse gasps. When it saw the little group on the law it lunged forward joyfully, almost pulling Caleb off his feet. Caleb at eighteen was just over six feet tall, built like a football player, and resembled his sister not at all, for his hair was blond and his eyes a warm, ingenuous brown. He dug his heels in the grass and leaned back on the rope, yelling, 'Whoa!' as if the dog were a team of huskies. The dog, to everyone's surprise, obeyed instantly, so that Caleb landed on his rump on the grass. Cecilia began to giggle. Said Sally, who knew her brother very well, 'We can't keep it, Caleb.'

Beside her Lynette murmured, 'You'd need a *very* rich husband to keep that dog.'

At the sound of their voices the dog sat down, head tilted to one side, his tongue lolling between businesslike white teeth. Caleb scrambled to his feet and said breathlessly, 'Look how well behaved he is. He'd make a great watch-dog.'

'He'd make a great donkey ride.'

'He was chained up behind the old garage. Lonnie was beating him.'

Lonnie was the local ne'er-do-well, reputed to beat his wife as well as his dog. Sally sighed, wishing not for the first time that Caleb were less soft-hearted. 'He's huge, Caleb—he'd eat more than you and me put together. We can't keep him, we can't afford it.'

'Yes, we can,' Caleb said eagerly, scratching the dog between its misshapen ears; it immediately assumed an expression of bliss. 'You see, I got two jobs this afternoon, sis. One working for your neighbours, Lynette—the Michaelsons. They want the house painted. And the other one doing gardening and splitting wood for the new people who've moved in at the far end of the peninsula; their name's Bartlett and they've got two kids. I did a couple of hours' work for them today.' He pulled a ten-dollar bill from his pocket. 'See? I could buy dog food with this.'

Lynette said, 'My boyfriend has a brother in the grocery business. I bet he could get me dog food at wholesale prices.'

'Lynette!' Sally scolded. 'The house is too small as it is, without adding that monstrosity.'

The dog flopped over on its back, looking like a moth-eaten rug. Its tail thumped the grass and its gigantic paws flailed the air. Cecilia rushed over to it, sat down on the grass and began tickling its belly. The paws stilled and the dog lay quietly, as if it sensed that Cecilia was small and consequently vulnerable. In spite of herself, Sally was impressed. 'It's probably loaded with fleas,' she said, her voice not quite as adamant as it had been.

'I could bathe him on the beach. Sal, I can't take him back to Lonnie and the only other choice is the pound. They put animals to sleep at the pound if they're not claimed in a few days.'

'Nobody else would claim him, that's for sure.' Sally scowled ferociously. 'Caleb, if we keep him you must promise not to bring home any more animals this

summer.' Inside the house were three cats, which had
arrived in varying states of decrepitude, and in a large
wire cage next to the shed lived a cold- eyed seagull
whose broken wing was nearly mended.

'I promise. Look how good he's being with Cecilia.'

Cecilia and the dog were gazing at each other with
eyes of love. Sally said in a resigned voice, 'What shall
we call him?'

We just studied Sir Philip Sidney in history class,'
Caleb said promptly. 'Let's call him Sidney.'

'I think Sir Philip Sidney was both better bred and
better groomed.'

'Give me time, sis, you won't recognise him a week
from now.'

Indeed a week did make a vast difference in Sidney's
appearance. Regular feeding filled in the hollows
between his ribs, bathing and brushing gave his fur a
cavalier sheen, and his perpetual grin spoke volumes
about his preference for Sally's house over Lonnie's
garage. Caleb did not bring home as much as an injured
sparrow all week.

Sally was working hard on a research paper for a
professor at St Mary's, the payment for which would
transform the new washing machine from dream to
reality. Dennis had taken her for a pleasant drive and a
lobster dinner on Saturday; the lilies of the valley were
in bloom in her garden; life was good. And then
Lynette phoned.

'Sally, guess what? Your holiday's on!'

Sally was seated at the word-processor entering a
very complicated sentence about the psycho-symbolic
propensities of Canadian literature. She said blankly,
'What holiday?'

'Your holiday. The one you promised to take.
Remember?'

Sally did remember. 'I told you I couldn't afford——'

'This will hardly cost you a cent. Well, it will cost

you something, but when you hear what you're getting, it's a fabulous bargain! And just what you need.'

There was no stopping Lynette when she used that tone of voice. Sally pushed the save button and inwardly began to marshal all the various reasons she could not take a holiday. Lynette was saying excitedly, 'A friend of mine, Raoul Desroches, was booked to go to St Pierre and Miquelon in three days. You know, the islands off the coast of Newfoundland. But he just found out he has a job interview in Quebec City two days after he's supposed to arrive in St Pierre. It's a job he really wants. So he asked me if I knew anyone who'd like to use his tickets, he's going by boat and I think he said he had reservations at a *pension*, it's astoundingly cheap there, Sally, and if you can't find a Frenchman who's willing, then I give up!'

'Lynette, I can't——'

'I'm coming over.'

The receiver clicked in Sally's ear. She said a very pithy word and went into the kitchen to put the kettle on. But while she was waiting for the water to boil, she found herself walking into the living-room to the bookshelves. There had been an article on St Pierre in one of the local magazines recently. She flipped through the pile, found the right issue and opened it. There were photographs of fog-wreathed villages and fishing boats which would not have been out of place in Nova Scotia. But there were also brightly clad Basque dancers, solemn-looking *gendarmes*, squat Norman churches and narrow little streets: the flavour foreign, exotic, exciting. She had not had a holiday, a proper holiday, since before Cecilia was born. She tried to imagine herself walking those narrow streets, hearing French spoken all around her, going into the *bureau de poste* to buy stamps, into the *musée* to learn the history of this tiny outpost of France, and felt her heart quicken.

No responsibilities. No typing, no house, no child. No brother, no dog, no bad-tempered seagull. No neighbours knowing all her business. No Dennis wanting to marry her. Only herself. Alone. She had almost forgotten what it was like to be alone . . .

The kettle screamed in the kitchen and Lynette banged on the door. Sally came back to earth with a bump, the practical persona with which she had faced all the various crises of the past five years reasserting itself. She couldn't afford a holiday. And she couldn't leave Cecilia. So that was that.

As soon as she went in the kitchen Lynette pounced. 'I know what you're going to say—you can't afford it. Your fare is free, the *pension* is something like fourteen dollars a night, breakfast included, you can eat bread and cheese for lunch, so you'd only have to buy one meal a day. And I'll look after Cecilia for nothing—as long as Caleb feeds the dog.'

Sally poured the tea and put some peanut-butter cookies on a plate. 'I couldn't leave Cecilia—I've never done that before.'

'I'll stay all day and I won't let her out of my sight. And Caleb will be here—he's very responsible.'

'Maybe I could take her with me . . .'

'Sally darling, don't make a martyr of yourself! You'll only be gone eight or nine days.'

'Anyway, I can't afford to go, Lyn.'

'You can't afford not to, you'll never get the chance for such an interesting holiday so cheaply. Look, I worked out roughly what it would cost you.' Lynette pushed a piece of paper across the table to Sally.

The total was amazingly low. Sally had more than that amount in her savings account. 'It would be heaven to spend a few days by myself,' she confessed.

'By yourself!' Lynette sat up in her chair. 'You're going to find yourself a man there, Sarah Ruth Cowan, or else I'll tell Raoul you don't want the tickets!'

'Blackmail,' Sally snorted.

'You're darn right. No use fighting fair with you, you're too stubborn.'

Sally cupped her hands around her mug, staring down into the clear, weak tea. 'I've found myself thinking about what you said a week ago,' she admitted in a low voice. 'I guess I don't want to be alone for the rest of my life. I worry about what will happen to Caleb, he should go to university and be a vet or a psychiatrist or a doctor, but how can I afford that? And Cecilia should have a father, particularly if Caleb moves out.'

'And what about you?' Lynette said gently. 'You always end up last on the list, love.'

'I sometimes daydream about being married again,' Sally whispered. 'To someone the opposite of Bruce. Someone mature and loving and strong. I've never told you that before, have I? But you see, whenever I meet anyone who's at all a likely candidate—and I know just as well as you that Dennis isn't the man for me—I run in the opposite direction. I can't face the demands that would be made on me.'

'The sexual demands,' Lynette said softly.

Sally's eyes had filled with tears. 'That's right,' she gulped. 'I'm such a coward, Lyn.'

'You're one of the bravest women I know. Sally, if you did meet someone nice on this trip, and you could get into bed with him, I think it would do you the world of good.'

'Sounds like a prescription for the common cold. Take one man and get into bed,' Sally quavered.

'The alternative is to suffer with the cold.'

Sally met her friend's eyes squarely. 'You may be right about the affair, perhaps I do need one. But in all honesty I couldn't do that, Lyn. Have an affair with someone I just met? Someone I don't even know? I couldn't!'

'Get to know him first.'

'In a week? Come off it!'

A calculating look crossed Lynette's face. 'you're already on the Pill, so you wouldn't have to worry about getting pregnant.'

'Only for that minor health problem I had a little while ago,' Sally said defensively. 'And only for six months.'

'It doesn't matter why you're taking them—they'll work just the same.'

Exasperated, Sally said, 'They won't have the chance! I'm not having an affair, Lyn. Not with Dennis, not with some man I meet on the streets of St Pierre! Do you hear me?'

'I think you're crazy, muddle-headed and wrong!' Lynette grumbled. 'But I suppose I could tell Raoul you'll use the tickets anyway.'

Sally raised her brows. 'Are you giving up that easily?'

'A holiday would do you good, you haven't had one in years. And you never know, you might meet Prince Charming on the first day and fall madly in love.'

'Pigs might fly,' Sally responded tartly. She did not want an affair, with Prince Charming or anyone else. Her conscience would have a hard enough time leaving Cecilia for a week. An affair was out of the question.

CHAPTER TWO

THREE days later, days of frantic and unremitting activity, Sally was ready to leave. By staying up until midnight two nights in a row, she had finished the professor's paper. She had cleaned the house from top to bottom and baked cookies and pies, honest enough to admit part of her motivation was guilt that she was leaving her family. She had washed and ironed clothing belonging to herself, Cecilia and Caleb. She had bought a tiny French dictionary.

She had also expended considerable effort preparing Cecilia for her departure. But on her last evening, when she had shown Lynette the clothes she was taking and had prevented Tigger the cat from climbing into her suitcase, she heard herself say, 'Lynette, I shouldn't be leaving Cecilia!'

Lynette rolled her eyes. 'I knew this would happen,' she said. 'Cecilia is a secure and happy little girl who's more excited about the present you're bringing her than she is about you leaving. Now go and put her to bed and then we'd better head out. Move it!'

Sally's brain told her Lynette was right; but her heart told her otherwise. She bathed her daughter and read her a story, then kissed her goodnight with a huge lump in her throat. She got out of the room without crying, hugged Caleb fiercely, muttering past the lump, 'Look after yourself, I'll be home in just over a week,' and ran out of the door. Lynette had already put her suitcase in the boot. As they drove down the winding little lane to the main road,

Lynette wisely kept silent.

They rounded the roundabout and headed downtown. It was eight o'clock and the ship was due to sail at nine-thirty. The fog had moved in from the sea, creating orange haloes around the lights on the waterfront, softening the utilitarian lines of the warehouses and grain elevators. Peering through the windscreen Lynette said with a grunt of satisfaction, 'That's the one—Pier thirty-six. That blue ship must be the one you're going on.' She grinned at Sally. 'Got your Gravol pills?'

The ship was dwarfed by a row of wheat silos. 'I may need them,' Sally said nervously. 'It says *Miquelon* on the side—must be the right boat.'

Lynette pulled up by the gangplank with a flourish, got out of the car and passed Sally her suitcase. 'Have a wonderful holiday,' she said, kissing Sally on the cheek. 'And you'll have to let me know when you get back whether Frenchmen deserve their reputation as lovers.'

'They'll have to earn their reputation with someone other than me,' Sally announced. 'I'm looking forward to a whole week of solitude.'

Lynette groaned. 'You're hopeless!'

'I can't go to a strange place and pick up a strange man and go to bed with him, Lyn—no way.'

Lynette gave her a look of exasperated fondness. 'All right, all right,' she said. 'But have a good time anyway, OK?'

'I will. Take care of Cecilia, won't you?'

'You don't have a worry in the world—just have fun.'

After that, there seemed nothing more to say. Sally picked up her case and trudged up the metal gangplank, which swayed slightly to her weight; the strip of water between the dock and the ship was a sinister, oily black. At the top of the gangplank she waved goodbye and watched Lynette drive off. She then found herself quite alone on the grey-painted deck of the ship. The paint was freshly applied, beaded with moisture from the fog. She could hear the faraway moan of a foghorn, and, nearer, the clang of metal near the bow as cargo was loaded. From a doorway behind her came an excited gabble of French, the voices indisputably male. But not one of the owners of those voices seemed the slightest bit interested in her arrival. So much for the flock of Frenchmen that Lynette had expected to converge on her, Sally thought drily.

When she had crossed the deck, climbed over the step and entered the superstructure, which was warm and dry and very clean, she located the source of the voices: no fewer than six men crowded around the purser's officer having an enthusiastic argument. Although Sally had taken French in school, she decided very quickly that it had been no preparation for six contentious Frenchmen. She cleared her throat and said politely, 'Excusez-moi. Je suis passagère á St Pierre. Je m'appelle Sally Cowan mais j'ai le billet de Raoul Descroches.'

One of the men, who had a chestnut pigtail and a very brief T-shirt, dragged his attention away from the argument long enough to say, 'Ah, oui—Descroches. La cabine cinq.'

'Numéro cinq?' she repeated carefully. 'J'ai le billet, m'sieur.'

'Ce n'est pas nécessaire.' He gave her a practised smile of undoubted charm and, waving his arms wildly, plunged back into the discussion.

She had worried a little that there might be a problem because Raoul's name was on the ticket rather than her own; she had obviously worried unnecessarily. The crew of the Miquelon could not care less. She walked down the narrow passageway,

checking the varnished cabin doors for number five,
already aware of an intoxicating sense of anonymity.
No one here knew who Sally Cowan was. No one
cared. For the space of nine days she could be anyone
she liked.

The door of cabin number five was propped open.
With faint dismay Sally saw that it was a double cabin,
two bunks one on top of the other. A haversack had
been dumped on the bottom bunk but there was no
other sign of the unknown occupant.

She would have preferred a room to herself. She was
not used to sharing sleeping-space; had not done so
since the brief months of her marriage to Bruce.

However, the cabin itself pleased her immensely. The
bunks were neatly made up with clean white sheets
and red wool blankets, there was a built-in desk, a
basin, and double wardrobes. A porthole gave her a
constricted view of the nearest pier. When she went to
bed tonight the ship would be out at sea, Sally thought
with a surge of excitement.

She took her sweater out of the suitcase, then put the
case in one of the wardrobes. Shrugging the sweater on
over her shirt, she put her rain-jacket back on and
decided to go up on deck to watch the boat leave the
dock.

On her way to the stern of the ship she almost
bumped into a couple entwined around each other and
kissing passionately. They were oblivious to her
presence; she would be willing to bet she was not
sharing her cabin with either of them. Two elderly
women weighed down with camera equipment were
chattering away about apertures and filters as they
photographed a freighter by the next pier. A middle-
aged couple smiled at her pleasantly, introducing
themselves as Bev and Dunc Cuthbert from Illinois, and
as she chatted to them she noticed two bronzed young
men striking up a conversation with two young women

in very tight jeans who were leaning against the railing on the next level. None of the people she could see seemed a candidate for her cabinmate.

She watched with the Cuthberts as the gangplank was pulled up and folded against the side of the ship. A dockhand flung the hawsers up on the deck, where the pigtailed crewman coiled them around thick metal posts. The underlying rumble of the engine deepened as the strip of water between the ship and the concrete dock began to widen. It was almost dark.

Fascinated, Sally forgot about her elusive cabinmate. As the *Miquelon* left the shelter of the pier and moved out into the harbour she saw the steady beam of the lighthouse on George's Island and the cluster of yellow lights on a moored oil-rig near the Dartmouth shore. The water was smooth and slick, split into a V by the bow. Marker buoys flashed red and green, and the blare of the foghorn was louder.

The Cuthberts went inside to find some coffee. Sally stayed by the railing, gazing out to sea, her hands in her pockets, the slight wind of the ship's motion stirring her hair. She felt as light and free as that breeze. She felt like an explorer leaving safe harbour to discover the unknown. She felt wonderful.

Not until the fog grew thicker and closed in around the ship did Sally leave her post by the railing. Although the calm waters of the harbour had given way to the choppiness of the open sea, the slap of waves against the prow exhilarated her; she felt no need of the Gravol pills. She crossed the deserted deck and went inside, deciding to leave her jacket in the cabin and go in search of some coffee herself. Her cheeks flushed from the sea-wind, her hair curling damply, she pushed open the door of the cabin. A very large man, naked to the waist, was shaving in front of the little mirror over the basin.

'Oh!' said Sally. 'I'm sorry—I must have the wrong

cabin.'

She backed out in a hurry, pulling the door shut. But the brass number affixed to the varnish was a five. She blinked and looked again. It was still five. Five. *Cinq*. This was her cabin. She had not made a mistake.

She pushed open the door again and said pleasantly, 'I think you must be in the wrong cabin. This one is mine.'

The man's head swung around. From nose to chin he was swathed in shaving-cream; the rest of his face managed to look quite annoyed. 'No,' he said shortly. 'Cabin number five.'

The euphoria Sally had felt on the deck was rapidly disappearing. 'Then the purser must have made a mistake,' she said as politely as she could. 'I'll probably have to disturb you again in a few minutes to move my suitcase into another cabin.' She shut the door, making a face at the brass number. He needn't have been quite so abrupt. And the mistake was probably because she was using Raoul's ticket.

The purser's office was locked and no one came when she knocked on the door. She went back down the corridor to the dining-room, smiling at the Cuthberts who were sitting at a table reading and sipping coffee. The foursome she had noticed earlier was getting rather noisily drunk at another table. She poked her head around the galley door. The pigtailed crewman was standing there, reflectively scratching his belly; he broke off his low-voiced conversation with the chef to give her a lazy smile. '*Madame*?'

Trying to be as tactful as she could, she said, '*Je pense qu'il y a une erreur. Il y a un homme dans ma cabine.*'

The lazy smile approached a leer. '*Oui*?'

Blushing, Sally said overloudly, '*Je ne veux pas——*' She broke off. What was the word for share? '*Je ne veux pas partager ma cabine avec un homme inconnu. Quelle autre cabine est inoccupée*?'

'*Pas une seule,*' he said impatiently.

'None?' she squeaked, forgetting her French.

He said with exaggerated slowness, as if she were mentally retarded, '*Toutes les cabines sont occupée, madame. Pas de choix.*'

'*Mais je ne veux pas——*'

He said something so rapidly she could not catch it. The chef laughed. Then he added with a small bow, '*Je m'excuse, madame, bonne nuit,*' took the chef by the arm and left by the far door.

Furious, Sally took one step after him. But she had as little desire to end up in the crew's quarters as she had to share the cabin with the large man who had been shaving. She backed out of the galley. The Cuthberts, who might possibly have come to her rescue, had gone, and the foursome, waving cognac bottles, had begun to sing. No help there.

She went back down the corridor, her mouth set in a grim line, tapped on the door of cabin five and walked in. The man had finished shaving and was now brushing his teeth. The water gurgled in the sink. She waited until he had finished and said frostily, 'There aren't any other empty cabins.'

He wiped his face with a towel, folded the towel and hung it over the rail. This gave Sally the time to have a good look at him. He had thick, dark brown hair with a slight wave to it; dark hair curled over his torso, which was impressively muscled. His eyes, had he been smiling, could also have been impressive, because they were the clear turquoise-blue of the water in the cove on a sunny day. But because he was not smiling, they were cold, distant and unfriendly, like the ocean on a day in February when the temperature is below zero. His chin, no longer hidden by shaving-cream, was determined, the nose strong, the eyes deep-set: a face full of strength and character, Sally thought, but by no means an approachable face.

With a quiver along her nerves she noticed something else. A thin white scar ran the length of the man's left forearm. Another scar, wider, curved around his ribs. From being merely unfriendly and unapproachable, he suddenly became downright dangerous. She did not want to share a cabin with a man who'd been involved in drunken brawls, who looked as if he was perfectly capable of murdering her in her sleep. Matters were not helped when he said coldly, 'Have you finished staring?'

There was some justice to his accusation. 'I'm sorry,' Sally said as pleasantly as she could, for she had decided it might be wise not to antagonise him. 'I didn't mean to stare. But it's not every day I find myself sharing a room with a total stranger.' She gave him what she hoped was a disarming smile, as innocent and cherubic as one of Cecilia's. 'It's not a situation I feel very comfortable with. I spoke to one of the crew members, but my French isn't very good—I'm sure they'd pay more attention to you than to me.' She paused hopefully.

'But he told you there weren't any other cabins. So why should I bother going to see him?'

The man's voice was brusque. Sally kept her smile pinned to her face. 'Because you're a man,' she said lightly. 'I'm sure they'd let you share with one of the crew.'

'Listen, Miss—I don't even know your name.'

For a moment she thought of saying Madame Descroches, of keeping her own identity hidden from this formidable man, but abandoned her impulse as an impracticality. 'Sally Cowan,' she said; her jaws were beginning to ache from smiling.

'I'm Luke Sheridan.' He did not offer to shake hands. 'I don't want to bunk in with a crew-member, Miss Cowan. I don't particularly want to share a cabin with you, either—I came on holiday to get away from

everyone, not to share my room with a complete
stranger. But this cabin is very comfortable, far more so
than the crew's cabins, I'm sure, and I should think for
two nights we can manage to keep out of each other's
hair. So if I were you I'd stop making such a fuss.'

Sally abandoned the smile. 'I am not making a fuss!'

'No?' As he leaned down and lifted his haversack
from the bottom bunk, putting it on the floor by the
basin, the overhead light shone on the smooth play of
muscles in his back. 'If it's your reputation you're
worried about, I promise I'll never tell anyone we spent
two nights together.'

'I can look after my own reputation, thank you very
much! And we are *not* spending the night——'

Sally broke off in mid-sentence. Her jaw dropped.

She thought of Lynette. Had Lynette purposely
engineered this situation, there could not have been a
more perfect opportunity for Sally to have an affair. For
the next two nights she was sharing her cabin with a
man. A man Lynette would undoubtedly call a hunk.
Certainly a presentable enough man for this much-
talked-of affair.

With a grunt of satisfaction Luke Sheridan pulled a
book out of his haversack and stood up. 'What's
wrong?' he said sharply.

'Nothing! Nothing at all,' Sally gabbled, and willed
herself not to blush.

'Look, Sally Cowan,' he said forcefully. 'I'm sure
you're a very nice woman, but I am not the slightest bit
interested in you. So for God's sake try and pretend I'm
your brother or your uncle or even a piece of the
furniture, if that'll help. We'll be together in this cabin
for sixteen hours at the most, and for most of those
sixteen hours, we'll be asleep. And I promise once we
dock we'll never see each other again. Does that make
you feel better?'

She was still gaping at him like a fish out of water.

Lynette had spent five minutes one afternoon describing Sally's mythical lover: attractive, easygoing, friendly and willing. A domesticated cat, thought Sally now. Whereas the *Miquelon* had presented her with a puma. Certainly she had immense difficulty seeing Luke Sheridan as anyone's uncle or brother. Let alone a piece of furniture. Danger, her nerves screamed. Run. But where could she run? To the crew's cabins? From the fat to the fire?

'I asked if you were feeling better,' Luke Sheridan repeated, an edge to his voice.

'Yes,' she gulped in total untruth. 'Thank you.'

'Good.' He glanced from one bunk to the other and said in a practical voice, 'As you're considerably smaller than me, would you mind taking the top bunk? If I sat up in it, I'd bang my head.'

'Sure. Sure, that would be fine.'

'Then if you'll turn your back for a minute, I'll get in bed. I think I'll read for a while. I've done a hell of a lot of overtime the last week and I'm tired.'

He had not taken a pair of pyjamas out of the haversack along with the book. Sally turned her back, staring fixedly at the door. Because her ears were already attuned to the steady throb of the ship's engine, she had no trouble hearing the sound of his zipper, the creak of the wardrobe door as he presumably hung up his trousers, the soft rustle of the sheets and blankets as he got into bed. Intimate sounds, indistinguishable from those Bruce used to make as he got ready for bed. Sally screwed up her eyes, trying to banish memories she did not want.

There was a little snap as Luke turned on the light over his bunk. 'OK,' he said.

'I'm going to the bathroom,' she gasped, and made her escape.

The bathroom, like the rest of the ship, was very clean. However, it contained only the basics and gave

her no excuse to linger. When she went back in to the
cabin, Luke Sheridan did not even look up from his
book. He had pulled the covers part-way up his chest.
But his shoulders and arms were bare.

Quickly looking away, Sally bent to undo her case.
But when she lifted the lid she frowned in puzzlement.
A large paper bag was lying on top of her carefully
arranged clothes. It had not been there when Sally had
closed the case. An envelope was taped to the bag, her
name written on it in Lynette's handwriting.

Luke Sheridan was temporarily forgotten. Sally
opened the envelope, pulled out the card and read,

> Darling Sally,
> I'm still hoping! So I took out that disgustingly prim
> nightdress you'd packed and substituted this one—I
> have great faith in the power of a sexy gown. Have
> fun! Love,

> Lynette

Inside the bag was a satin nightgown a soft shade of
apricot, edged with lace. Sally fumbled through the rest
of her clothes. Her white cotton nightshirt, floor-length,
ruffled at the throat and wrists, was gone.

Not knowing whether to laugh hysterically or burst
into tears, Sally pulled the satin gown from the bag.
Even without trying it on she could see that the slits in
the hem and the plunging neckline would be, to put it
mildly, revealing.

She had not packed a housecoat.

Inwardly cursing Lynette, Sally took the apricot gown
from the bag. She shot a hunted glance at the lower
bunk. Luke Sheridan was absorbed in his book,
frowning slightly as he turned a page. It was Umberto
Eco's *Name of the Rose*, whose plot was complicated
enough to claim his attention over any number of sexy
nightgowns. She hoped. But the bunks were built in
such a way that he had a view of the entire cabin. There

was nowhere for her to hide, and she certainly couldn't
change in the bathroom and saunter down the corridor
in a garment designed to drive any man worthy of the
name mad with lust. She said in a strangled voice,
'Close your eyes please, Mr Sheridan.'

He looked up. 'As you're going to be sleeping two
feet over my head, I think we should dispense with
formality—the name is Luke. And stop looking like a
frightened rabbit. You're not my type.'

For a moment Sally forgot the dilemma of the
nightgown. 'What's wrong with me?' she demanded.

'Nothing,' he said irritably, 'I shouldn't have said
that, I'm sorry. Get in your pyjamas and go to bed.'
And he ostentatiously closed his eyes.

So he thought she was a frightened rabbit, did he?
Not his type. Abruptly a much younger Sally surfaced,
the rebellious girl who had defied her mother to go to
dances and stay out late. How dared Luke Sheridan
compare her to a rabbit! She'd show him.

Quickly Sally took off all her clothes, hanging them
on the rail in the wardrobe, and then slid the gown over
her head. She looked down at herself. The edge of the
lace was fractionally above her nipples. The slits in the
hem came to mid-thigh. But why should she worry?
She wasn't his type. She closed the wardrobe door and
said politely, 'Thanks, Luke.'

In what was probably instinctive good manners, he
looked up. With great satisfaction Sally saw his eyes
widen and the book drop to his chest, and added, 'Shall
I switch off the overhead light?'

Although the light was shining full on her, she did
not realise quite how devastating she looked. The
apricot shade of the gown warmed her skin; her hair
was an aureole about her head, her eyes a luminous
grey.

Luke Sheridan said nothing, nor did he pick up his
book. So she reached behind her to the switch by the

door, a move which shadowed her cleavage and exposed the slim line of her legs, and turned out the light. The semi-darkness giving her courage, she walked to the end of the bunk and said cordially, 'I think you'd better close your eyes again, I can't imagine how I'm going to climb this ladder with any semblance of decency.'

Again he did not reply. Sally hitched up the hem of the gown and climbed the wooden ladder with as much grace as was possible. She crawled up the bunk, got under the covers and said, 'Goodnight, Luke. Enjoy your book.'

There was a small silence. 'Goodnight,' he said, with undeniable grimness.

Sally smiled to herself. Lynette would be proud of her. She was not sharing Luke's bunk, of course, and had no intention of doing so; but she had definitely dispelled any notions of rabbits. She curled up on her side, closing her eyes. To the rhythm of the engines and the slow sway of the ship on the swell, she fell asleep.

She was lying on a beach in the hot sun beside a dark-haired man whose arms were scarred; the waves splashed gently on the sand . . .

Sally opened her eyes, discovering that the sun was the overhead light and the waves the sound of Luke Sheridan brushing his teeth in the white porcelain basin. She pulled the red wool blanket up to her chin, embarrassed to have had a dream so full of sensual warmth. 'What's the time?' she muttered.

'Ten past eight. Breakfast at eight-thirty.'

He had not said good morning. He had not asked if she had slept well. 'Bacon and eggs would go down well,' she said.

'As this is a French ship I'm sure it will be a Continental breakfast. Rolls and coffee.'

'Is that all?'

'That's all.'

She would wager a considerable sum of money that Luke was pleased to be able to disappoint her. She gave an exaggerated yawn. 'I haven't been able to sleep past eight o'clock for five years. So I'm certainly not getting up for rolls and coffee.'

'Suit yourself.'

'Make sure I'm up in time for lunch, though.'

He had been combing his hair and now turned to face her. 'I am taking no responsibility for getting you out of that bunk, Sally Cowan.'

Because he was tall, his eyes were almost on a level with hers; they looked no friendlier than they had last night. Sally said with great interest, 'Are you always bad-tempered in the mornings?'

'Not when I'm alone.'

'No one to be bad-tempered with?'

'No reason to be bad-tempered.'

There was, finally, a glint of humour in his eyes. She said, 'That's better—you look almost human.'

The glint disappeared. 'And what do I look the rest of the time?'

'Inhuman, obviously . . . I should never have started this conversation.'

'Smartest thing you've said so far.

She scowled at him and had no trouble coming up with more adjectives. 'Also unapproachable, unfriendly, and if you'll excuse me for sounding melodramatic, a little bit dangerous.'

She had the feeling she had struck home. He said tightly, 'You and my boss would get along well . . . I'll take my book and my jacket so I won't have to disturb you again.' He gave her a curt nod. 'Lunch is served at noon.'

As he closed the cabin door behind him, Sally pulled a face. She was perfectly safe as far as this mythical affair was concerned, for not by the wildest stretch of her imagination could she imagine herself seducing Luke Sheridan. On the basis of two brief conversations she was quite sure he could not be coerced into anything against his will. And she, as he had said, was not his type. He would go for tall sophisticated blondes who smoked cigarillos and would never be foolish enough to get pregnant. Blondes with modern Swedish furniture and executive-level jobs and white sports cars. Blondes who would wear brief satin nightgowns. Or nothing at all.

Sally thumped her pillow and turned her face to the wall. She might be safe as far as sexual involvement was concerned. But Luke did have a very strange effect on her. He made her feel wilful and very much alive, arousing feelings she had had to subdue since Cecilia was born. Maybe holidays were dangerous, she thought soberly. Maybe she had become a different person by getting away from all the responsibilities of home: in walking up the gangplank she had crossed more than a narrow strip of black water. But she could not afford to change, because in only a few days she had to go home and pick up all the strands of her life again.

She gave the pillow another thump and closed her eyes. She was not going to spoil her holiday by such morbid reflections. To hell with Luke Sheridan and the effect he had on her. Some time tomorrow the boat would dock and she need never see him again. Him and his frightened rabbits and his sexy blondes.

She pulled the covers over her head and very methodically began listing all the flowers in her garden. She had reached Salvia and Scabiosa before she went to sleep.

CHAPTER THREE

AT noon Sally was in the dining-room sharing a table with the Cuthberts and the two grey-haired camera enthusiasts, whose names were Helen and Bertha. Luke came in ten minutes later and sat down with the young tourists who were now firmly a foursome; covertly she watched him talking and laughing. Charming them, she thought irritably. He had not considered *her* worth charming.

However, the lunch was delicious, a thick country soup served with pâté, smoked fish, home-made bread and a *salade vinaigrette*. Sally had always liked to eat, and it transpired that the two elderly ladies had made several trips to the Arctic, a part of Canada she had often wanted to visit.

Her table was finished before Luke's. He was in the middle of telling what sounded like a very funny story and did not acknowledge her presence as she walked past. She got her sweater and jacket out of the cabin and went up on deck.

The mist was so thick that the ship was isolated in a small circle of steel-grey water; had it not been for the wake at the stern, they might not have been moving. She stared at the impenetrable wall of fog, wondering where they were, missing Cecilia, wishing the child were beside her, small hand clasped with her own.

A crew-member wearing a navy-blue duffel coat, a knit cap pulled down over his ears, clumped down the deck towards her. His face was chubby and wind-burned. He smiled at her, asking her in heavily accented English if she would like to go up to the

bridge. She accepted with pleasure, because she did
not want to think about Cecilia, and introduced
herself. His name was Jacques Lefèvre. He was a St
Pierrais.

Although the workings of the steering and the
radar remained mysteries to Sally, she discovered
that the vessel was pulling away from the coast of
Cape Breton to head across the Gulf of St Lawrence
towards Newfoundland, and that they would arrive
in St Pierre early the next morning. She also
discovered that their cargo had been transferred off
big container ships from Le Havre. On a more
mundane level, she found out that Jacques had a wife
whom he obviously adored and a son named Paul
Antoine Alexandre, aged seven months. So she was
able to talk about Cecilia, and left the bridge warmed
by the human contact.

She went to stand by the rail at the stern, where the
clean white foam of the wake churned and tumbled
and splashed. There was something hypnotic about
the grey-green waves that followed the ship in tidy
procession, to be finally smothered by the fog. She
had enjoyed talking to Jacques, she thought, and had
found it easy to tell him about Cecilia. Because he was
married and therefore safe? She could not imagine
telling Luke Sheridan about Cecilia. He, she felt sure,
was not married. *He* sent tiny prickles of alarm along
her nerve endings, warnings to beware of
involvement. Lynette was right. She was afraid of
men like Luke Sheridan.

She frowned at the water. Bruce had never been
violent with her, had never beaten or abused her in
any way that she could publicly have complained of.
But even in the few months they had been together
she had grown to dread the nights that he had
wanted to make love to her. He had not been cruel,
no. But he had been demanding and unimaginative

and selfish, caring for his own pleasure rather than hers; faults of youth, she had since thought, wanting to excuse him. Because, of course, she had been young too, and burdened with an unwanted pregnancy, in no state to be able to assert herself or make sexual demands of her own. She was not sure he would have listened, anyway. Bruce had not wanted to marry her. He had seen her as a trap, as the person who had ended the careless hedonism of his teenage years. Perhaps sex, for him, had been a means of venting hostility rather than love.

She would probably never know the answer to that. What she did know was that Bruce had left her with a lasting aversion to the sexual act. She had found it subtly demeaning, sometimes painful, always unsatisfying; and while her reason might tell her that Bruce was only one man among many and that with other men she might enjoy making love, her emotions could not make that leap. She had met a number of men over the past four years, mostly through her work, and many of them had been single and several had been interested in her, but each and every one she had discouraged. The question Lynette had raised was whether she wanted to do that for the rest of her life. Did she want to remain single and alone, bereft of the companionship a man could offer because she was afraid of sex?

A seabird, black and white, skimmed the waves behind the ship and then vanished into the fog: as transitory an appearance as any of the men in her life, she thought wryly. Except for Dennis. But Dennis was safe, because he never made sexual demands on her.

She was not ready for an affair, she thought sombrely. No matter that Lynette had said she should overcome her fears. No matter that she did not want to be alone for ever. She was simply not ready.

This was no doubt a valid conclusion. But perhaps

it was not the moment for a familiar voice to say behind her, 'You look deep in thought. I trust you're not contemplating jumping overboard?'

Maybe because Luke had startled her, she heard herself say, 'I've never contemplated doing that. Not even in the worst of times.'

'So you've had bad times, have you?' Luke said thoughtfully. 'You look too young.'

Hastily Sally tried to steer the conversation towards generalities. 'I don't think youth gives one any immunity. I don't think anything does.'

'I have to agree. So what caused the worst of times for you?'

She had had time to collect herself. 'Luke,' she said carefully, 'you've really given me no reason to confide in you.'

'I suppose I haven't.' His eyes narrowed. 'We kind of got off on the wrong foot, didn't we? I came on holiday looking for solitude, and I gather you did the same, and then we got stuck in the same cabin. A situation I handled with something less than grace.'

'Me, too,' she admitted, and gave him a rueful smile.

She was standing with her back to the rail. He said abruptly, 'Your eyes are the same colour as the sea, do you know that?'

'Dirty green?'

He smiled. It transformed his face, ridding him of his formidable air of self-containment. 'That's not what I meant at all. And you know it.'

If one of Lynette's prerequisites for the imaginary lover was that he be attractive, Luke Sheridan more than filled the bill, Sally thought dazedly. Wanting to keep the smile on his face, she said, 'So what did you mean?'

He stepped closer to her, resting a hand on the railing beside her. 'They're depthless, a shade somewhere between grey and green. Although, unlike the sea, they have little rust flecks in them. The colour of your hair.'

'Rust is a very polite word to use for the colour of my hair.'

'I was brought up to be polite. Would you prefer orange?'

'Rust will do nicely, thank you,' Sally responded, thinking what an odd conversation this was and wondering why she was enjoying it so much.

Luke put his head to one side. 'A sort of pumpkin colour?'

She laughed. 'More like marigolds.'

'Or carrots.'

'Or cooked lobster.'

It was his turn to laugh. 'That won't do at all. Do you know what it's really like?' He reached out and took a single damp tendril between his fingers; inwardly she trembled at the intensity in his face. 'It's like flame. The glowing coals at the heart of a fire. Vivid. Alive. A man could warm his hands at it.'

Sally stood very still. No one had ever said such things to her before, let alone a man with the magnetism of Luke Sheridan. Her mother had kept her hair very short, as if to minimise its effect. Bruce had been apt to call her Carrots. Dennis had once told her she should put a rinse on it to tone it down. No one had ever likened it to the fierceness of fire. In a flash of insight she suddenly saw her hair as a symbol of herself. Did she want to be subdued and laughed at and toned down? Or did she want to be fully alive, glowing with glorious colour . . . a woman whom a man could love? A place where he could warm his hands?

In what seemed like a single smooth movement Luke dropped his hand from her hair and stepped back. 'If I'm not being rude to you, I'm being embarrassingly romantic,' he said with a lightness belied by the guarded features. 'I apologise for both.'

Sally felt as if someone had given her a gorgeous

bouquet of roses and then snatched the flowers away before she could touch the velvet petals or inhale their fragrance. 'You didn't mean what you said?'

'Of course I meant it. I shouldn't have said it, that's all.'

She replied with careful truth, 'I'm as out of my depth with you as if I *had* jumped overboard.'

'Then I think we'd better talk about the weather.'

Valiantly she played along. 'Marine forecasters call this zero visibility.'

'I hope the radar's working.'

'Oh, it is.' And she relayed her conversation with Jacques. This led to Luke telling her about a particularly harrowing journey he had taken on a yacht along the coast of Maine. He finished by asking, 'Have you sailed at all, Sally?'

'Never,' she said wistfully. 'I've been out in fishing boats a few times, but never on a yacht. They always look so beautiful to me, so free . . . oh well, maybe some day.'

Luke said, almost roughly, 'I get the feeling there have been quite a few some days in your life.'

Some day I'd like to be married to someone mature and loving and strong . . . Sally blushed and said, 'Instant gratification isn't supposed to be good for you.'

'Infinitely delayed gratification isn't good for you, either.'

He, of course, had no inkling of her fear of men. But it was as if he were speaking directly to all her doubts and delaying tactics and telling her to rid herself of them. To act now. In the present.

Sally had no idea what she would have said next. But walking slowly, arms around each other, the couple she had privately labelled the honeymooners came towards them along the deck, as encased in their own private world as the ship was in the mist; they certainly seemed unaware of Luke and Sally, because they stopped in the shelter of a doorway and kissed with an explicitness that made Sally uncomfortable. She turned away, rather hoping Luke had not seen them.

'They must be newly married,' she muttered.

'I doubt it—or if they are married, it's probably not to each other.'

'What a cynical thing to say!'

'Not cynical—realistic.'

'I don't want to believe that of them.'

He seemed to realise he had genuinely distressed her. Patting her sleeve he said, 'That's sweet of you, Sally. Far be it from me to disillusion you. I'm going to go inside, I promised myself I'd finish that book before we land in St Pierre. See you later.'

As she watched him stride down the deck, her face was troubled. What a strange mixture he was of intuition and impatience, enthusiasm and cynicism. When he had described the yachting trip to her his voice had rung with a young man's love of adventure; but a deep bitterness had fuelled his comment on the honeymooners. She did not understand him, she knew that. But she was beginning to like him.

Danger, she thought uneasily. Danger . . . because tonight she would again be sharing the cabin with him.

When Sally went for dinner that night, Luke was sitting with the Cuthberts, who waved to her to join them. Briefly Sally hesitated. But in the crowded, noisy dining-room it was hard to see Luke as any threat to her. She smiled and sat down at their table.

Dunc said amiably, 'Don't you look pretty.'

She was wearing grey slacks and a handknit jade-green sweater, and the sea air had put colour in her cheeks. 'Thank you!' she said, and because Dunc was perfectly safe she gave him her most generous smile.

Dunc leaned over the table. 'Right pretty,' he repeated. 'Wouldn't you agree, Luke?'

Luke's voice sent frissons along Sally's spine. 'Sure,' he said, 'very pretty,' and raised his glass in mocking salute.

Hastily Sally took a gulp of her own wine and began making rather frantic conversation with Bev. The food was excellent, *canard à l'orange* and the most delicious baked potatoes she had ever eaten in her life, accompanied by liberal amounts of full-bodied if rather rough red wine, and followed by strong black coffee. Then a large bottle of cognac appeared on their table. Dunc, without asking, poured generous amounts in each of the four glasses. 'Dirt cheap,' he said, unabashedly loosening his belt and settling back on the bench. He was wearing a baby-blue knitted shirt under a striped blazer, and his pink-cheeked face still had something of the innocence of a baby. 'Wouldn't want to tell you what we pay for a bottle of that particular brand back home in Peoria, Illinois. Taxes. That's what it is. They're ruining us.' He swirled the cognac in its bulb-shaped glass and took a hefty swallow.

'Now, Dunc,' said his wife, 'don't you get started on taxes or the government, these nice people don't want to hear about that.'

Sally had the feeling that Bev Cuthbert would see most of the world as nice people. Not even Luke could be cynical about their marriage, Sally decided, for while it was plain Bev and Dunc knew each other through and through, it was also plain they adored each other. Luke seemed to become gentle in their presence, to lose his hard edge, and Sally heard herself being wittier than usual, sparkling in conversation in a way that would have amused Lynette.

The waiter removed the last of the dishes and wiped the table. Bev said brightly, 'We don't want to go back to the cabin yet, do we? Why don't we have a nice little game of cards?'

'I never learned to play bridge,' Sally said

apologetically; she was sure the Cuthberts must play bridge in Peoria, Illinois.

'We could play hearts, that's easy to learn.' Bev smiled at Sally. 'Or maybe you already know it.'

Because Sally's mother had disapproved of card games—as well as dancing, sex, drinking, and any number of other pursuits that might be called pleasurable—Sally's childhood and adolescence had of necessity been crimped. She murmured, 'No, I don't know how to play hearts—but I could learn,' and thought how her mother would have deplored this scene: Dunc leaning back smoking a cigar; Bev with her manicured fingers flashing diamonds; the bottle of cognac; the pack of cards. And Luke. Disturbingly attractive Luke with whom Sally was sharing a cabin.

'I'll explain the rules,' Dunc said firmly. 'You couldn't explain tic-tac-toe to a chess champion, honey.'

'Now, Dunc,' said Bev, not at all put out.

The game seemed straighforward enough to Sally. The aim was to end up with all the hearts and with the two and queen of spades, or with none of them: nothing in between. 'Sounds like fun,' she said.

And so it was. Bluff and guesswork were called for, as well as a good memory for the cards already played. Several times Sally outsmarted Luke, or saw that he had guessed her strategy and was about to outsmart her, and they exchanged glances of laughing complicity. Dunc played a safe game, keeping his score low by taking no risks, while Bev played with erratic brilliance, twice ending up with all the necessary cards, twice with all of them but a single heart. She was as good-natured a loser as a winner. And throughout all this the level of cognac in the dark green bottle sank lower and lower.

Sally had not had such fun in months. Because she did not have to worry about Cecilia or Caleb or any

other of her responsibilities, she felt young and
carefree; when she tried to picture Dennis as one of the
card players she failed utterly, and wondered if when
she got home she should stop seeing him, a thought
that rather pleased her; and finally she knew that she
liked Luke and Luke liked her. It was a heady
sensation. One of the problems in her marriage had
been that she had not liked Bruce, nor he her. Liking
was very important, she felt, and gave Luke another
incautious, brilliant smile.

At midnight Dunc yawned immensely and said,
'Time to quit, honey. We've got to be up bright and
early in the morning.' Rather smugly he regarded the
score-sheet. 'Seems as though I won.'

So those who play safe are the winners? Was that
really so? Sally wondered. She had played it safe for
four years now. But was she a winner? Lynette did not
think so.

She looked up and found Luke's eyes on her. A
hectic flush on her cheeks, she said, 'I believe we're
tied.'

He smiled. His dark hair was ruffled and his eyes
very blue. 'So we are,' he said. 'I'm going to stay here
and finish my cognac and read for a while.'

He was being tactful, not wanting to advertise to the
Cuthberts that he and Sally were sharing a cabin.
Gratefully Sally said, 'OK. Goodnight Bev, Dunc—that
was fun!'

She followed them down the corridor, gathered up
her toilet articles in the cabin, and had a shower. Fully
dressed, she went back to the cabin. Luke was still not
there. The shower had sobered her somewhat, enough
to remind her of the apricot nightgown. Quickly she
stripped off her clothes again and pulled the gown over
her head. The satin felt cold against her skin.

On impulse she walked over to the mirror above the
basin. There she saw a woman with shining grey eyes

and parted lips, whose ivory skin seemed to glow with a life of its own. And what a lot of skin one could see, Sally thought involuntarily. She might as well be naked.

She left the mirror with its image of a woman she scarcely knew, and began sliding her suitcase back in the wardrobe. The side strap caught on the latch. Wrestling with the heavy case, she missed the tap at the door. When it opened she was bent forward, her legs exposed to mid-thigh, her breasts almost falling out of her gown.

'Don't you own a housecoat?' Luke snapped.

Sally jumped, dropped the handle of the case and flushed scarlet. 'I didn't bring one.'

'You believe in flaunting your wares.'

His eyes were full of contempt, his change of mood absolute. Sally should have scuttled into her bunk and pulled the blankets over her head. Instead she said defiantly, 'Don't be crude.'

'There's nothing very subtle about that rig. Although I suppose it's a surefire way to catch a man. Is that what you're after, Sally Cowan?'

'No!'

'Sure you are,' he sneered, letting his gaze wander offensively over her cleavage. 'You're on the make—out for a holiday fling.'

She pulled at the lace, trying to cover her bosom, and thereby exposed more thigh. 'I am *not*—that's the last thing I want.'

'Why the hell can't you at least be honest about it? You're wearing a nightgown that wouldn't disgrace a prostitute, for God's sake!'

Had the circumstances been different Sally might have tried to explain Lynette's duplicity. But Luke was standing scarcely six inches away from her, his eyes like chips of ice from a glacier, an immensity of anger in him as awesome as the glacier's power. Danger, her brain screamed. Wiling herself not to back up, she repeated, 'I am not looking for an affair,' and heard her voice quiver with strain.

'I don't believe you—you were waiting up for me, weren't you?'

This time her voice was overloud. 'I was trying to get my suitcase in the wardrobe!'

'And it got stuck just as I walked in the door?'

Sally did not have red hair for nothing; and during the past five years she had repressed a great deal of anger. 'You flatter yourself, Luke Sheridan—I wouldn't have an affair with you if you were the only man on this boat!'

'Oh, wouldn't you?' he said silkily. 'I wonder if I could change your mind.'

Her anger abandoned her, leaving her filled with fear. She backed against the wardrobe until the suitcase dug into her leg. 'Don't, Luke,' she stammered.

But he, if anything, was growing angrier. 'Why not? As Dunc so astutely remarked, you're right pretty. And your body isn't bad, either.' He looked her up and down in a way that seemed to strip her naked. 'Not bad at all.'

'*Stop it*!' Sally choked. She took a quick step sideways, intent upon reaching the ladder to her bunk. 'I'm going to bed.'

Luke moved with lightening speed, pinning her arms to her sides. 'Not yet, you're not.'

Her smoke-grey eyes met his cold blue ones in a fierce clash of wills. 'If you don't let go, I'll scream my head off!'

'Oh, will you? Will you really, Sally?' Very deliberately Luke let go of one arm and slid his hand across her shoulder, tracing the hollow of her collarbone, then letting his fingers move to her breast. He pushed the lace aside, cupping the soft swell of her flesh with its rose-pink tip, and all the while his eyes held her mesmerised.

For a full five seconds Sally was frozen in shock. Then, tumbling into her consciousness, came the searing heat of his fingers against her skin, their confidence as they caressed her nipple, their shameless certainty. Her whole body sprang to life like a flame leaping from grey ashes, ashes that might have appeared dead. Her eyes widened and her body subtly relaxed.

Cold water to the flame, Luke dropped his hands to his sides and said with scathing contempt, 'You're willing! You only met me yesterday and now you'd get in bed with me—wouldn't you?'

Sally crossed her arms over her breast, trying to still their trembling, everything in her nature torn apart by one brief, shattering caress. 'No, Luke, I wouldn't—I'm not like that,' she said. 'I don't believe in casual sex.' Which was the understatement of the year, she thought wildly.

'You're surely not telling me you're a virgin?'

She paled. 'No. I——'

'Good. That would have strained my credulity.'

She had never seen such bitterness in a man's face before. 'Why are you so angry?' she whispered.

'I loathe deceit. You flaunt yourself in that goddamned nightdress then have the nerve to tell me you're as pure as the driven snow?' He mimicked her savagely. *'An affair is the last thing I want . . .* I wasn't born yesterday, Sally.'

She thought of saying six times in rapid succession, 'I do not want an affair.' But she had the feeling Luke would not hear a word she said. Strangely the depth of anger in him had ceased to threaten her, for it revealed a great deal about him; and she discovered in herself, as unpredictably as that brief flame of desire, a need to know more.

Her silence seemed to infuriate him. 'Why do you

want a man—adding another notch to your belt?'

Sally shook her head and answered with gentle irony, 'I didn't bring a belt with me.'

'Bored with your husband, then? Want to have a little fling?'

He was shaking her, although she was sure he was unconscious of his actions. 'I don't have a husband,' she said roundly.

'So perhaps you're into motherhood,' Luke snarled. 'That's all the rage these days, isn't it? Have a baby and raise it on your own without benefit of a husband—is that what you want, Sally?'

Her sense of humour bubbled to the surface. 'Definitely not. You haven't answered my question, Luke.'

'Oh, the answer's no.' He suddenly released her and stepped back, rubbing his palms along the sides of his trousers as if he wished to remove all traces of her from his skin. 'I won't have an affair with you. I thought you would have guessed that by now.'

'Let us be accurate here,' Sally replied with careful precision. 'I never asked you to have an affair with me. I asked why you're so angry.'

Briefly Luke looked disconcerted. 'If you'll forgive the pun, that's surely my affair,' he retorted.

'Very funny. So you're not going to tell me?'

'No. It's none of your business.'

She was not quite ready to give up. 'You mean you can throw all sorts of personal questions at me but I can't do the same? Why don't *you* want an affair, Luke?'

'That's not your business, either.' He turned away from her dismissively, beginning to unbutton his shirt. 'I'm sure there are any number of men on this ship or in St Pierre who'd be delighted to take you to bed. But I'm not one of them.'

'You're married?'

'No.'

With immense satisfaction she saw she had him on the defensive. She pressed her advantage. 'So are you a misogynist, Luke? You hate all women?'

His breath hissed between his teeth. 'Lay off, Sally. All I said was that I don't want an affair with *you*.'

Sally flinched, for in those few words Luke had brought all her old inadequacies to the surface. She watched him hang up his shirt, almost against her will noticing the breadth of his shoulders and the tangle of dark hair on his chest, and said forlornly and quite without affectation, 'Am I so undesirable that you can't bear the thought of taking me to bed?'

'Don't be ridiculous.'

'I want to know the answer, Luke—it's important to me,' she said stubbornly.

'Sally, get into bed and go to sleep. This has gone on long enough.'

'You can't send me to bed like a naughty child! I'm a grown woman.'

Very deliberately he unzipped his cords, stepped out of them, and hung them neatly in the wardrobe. 'That, my dear, is part of the problem,' he said nastily.

He was wearing dark briefs and nothing else. Sally felt a twinge of fear and tried hard to hold on to her composure. 'I don't know what you mean.'

'Don't you?' Luke closed the distance between them in two short steps. 'Then I'll have to show you, won't I?'

She was once more made aware of how very much larger than she he was; his anger came from a source she could not begin to guess. If he touched her, would he again ignite that brilliant flame whose existence she had not even guessed? She said breathlessly, 'Luke——'

Roughly he put his arms around her, pulling her against the length of his body. Her hands were trapped at her sides; although she felt helpless and very frightened, she was determined not to lose what little dignity she had left by struggling. 'Let go,' she said coldly.

'I thought this was what you wanted.' He bent his head and kissed her, his mouth unyielding, his body like a cage imprisoning her.

It was a kiss full of anger, devoid of tenderness, surrendering nothing that was the essence of Luke. But some things he could not control nor Sally prevent: the warmth of her body where it touched his; the softness of her breasts against his chest; the tiny shock that ran through her when she felt his arousal. Violently he pushed himself away from her, his fists clenched at his sides. The harshness of his breathing and her own frantic, shallow breaths were all that could be heard over the monotonous drone of the engines.

Luke was the first one to speak. 'Does that answer the question of your desirability?' he grated.

Sally was a fighter. She had been ever since her first outraged screams in the delivery room; and she had needed to be to avoid being crushed by her mother's dour personality and inflexible rules. Although her face was pale and her body was trembling very lightly, like a leaf in the wind, she lifted her chin and said evenly, 'I believe it does. Although perhaps that kiss said more about you than about me.'

The overhead light fell mercilessly on every line in his face, and made caverns of the deep-set eyes. Without saying a word, Sally climbed the ladder to her bunk and drew the blanket up to her chin. Luke turned off the light. She heard the slap of his bare feet on the floor and the tiny sounds as he too got into bed. Then silence.

She lay very still, flat on her back; her feet were cold. But more than her feet were cold, for she felt chilled through and through by what had just happened between her and Luke in the narrow little cabin. He had been right: briefly, agonisingly, and against all the lessons of the past, she had been willing. A part of her nature that she had repressed for years had confronted her, and she was far too honest to deny that confrontation. Her sexuality was not dead. In a convoluted way Lynette's nightgown had served its purpose.

Luke had also wanted her. Against his will, maybe—but he had definitely wanted her. So why the anger? Why the corrosive bitterness, the contempt, the self-denial? She had no idea of the answers to any of these questions. But she knew one thing. She was not going to ask Luke himself. She had done enough damage for one night. When she got off the ship tomorrow morning she sincerely hoped she would never see Luke Sheridan again. That he was quite possibly lying in the bunk below her wishing the same thing about her was no comfort at all.

Dry-eyed, her body rigid in the bunk, Sally gazed into the darkness, until eventually the rhythmic rise and fall of the ship on the Atlantic waves sent her to sleep.

CHAPTER FOUR

SALLY woke several times in the night. But when the *Miquelon* docked in St Pierre at seven thirty the next morning she was fast asleep. She did not hear the steward's passage along the corridor as he tapped on the doors of all the cabins, nor did she hear Luke get out of bed and get dressed. She did not hear him call her name, the first time softly, the second time more insistently. She woke with a jump to a hand clasping her shoulder and shaking her. When she twisted in the bed, her eyes wide and startled, the first thing she saw Luke's face, almost at a level with her own. Everything that had happened the night before rushed back into her memory with horrible clarity; embarrassment and pain warred in her features as she stammered, 'What's wrong?'

Luke must have seen the misery in her grey eyes. He let go of her shoulder, stepped back and said with impersonal politeness, 'Nothing's the matter, Sally. But we've arrived in St Pierre and the customs officers are due on board in twenty minutes or so.'

Struggling up from a sleep that had been shot through with confused and menacing dreams, none of which she could remember, Sally registered only the coldness in Luke's face and his unspoken desire to be rid of her; a reality no more pleasant than her dreams. He added, 'We've been asked to take our luggage to the purser's office—so I'll get out of your way.'

He took a rain-jacket from the wardrobe, picked up his haversack and left the cabin. Suddenly aware of the silence, for the engines had stopped, Sally watched the

55

door shut behind him. To relieve her feelings she pulled a hideous face at it.

Then, because she could not stay in the bunk all day, much as she might have liked to, she crawled to the ladder, climbed to the floor and got dressed. She took her time, putting on extra make-up to hide the circles under her eyes and brushing her hair until it crackled with life. Only when she was satisfied that she looked like a carefree tourist enjoying her holiday did she close her case and leave the cabin.

The passengers were all crowded in the corridor. Luke was at the head of the line, talking to an official-looking gentleman in a blue uniform, who even as Sally watched handed Luke back some papers and waved him towards the door with a genial remark. Luke responded equally genially, heaved his haversack on his back, and stepped outside without a backward look. The honeymooners, their arms around each other, handed over their passports.

Feeling as removed from a carefree tourist as it was possible to feel, Sally took her place at the back of the line; by the time she left the ship, Luke would have vanished into the maze of narrow little streets that had so intrigued her in the magazine article. She had wanted him to disappear, hadn't she? So why did she feel like sitting down on her suitcase and crying her eyes out?

Fortunately, at this juncture Bev Cuthbert caught sight of Sally. She waved a beringed hand and called cheerfully, 'We'll wait for you, Sally—we can share a cab into town.'

Sally mouthed her thanks and wished she had woken early enough to get a mug of coffee from the galley; her stomach was growling. However, the line-up moved rapidly forward, and the customs officer, when her turn came, was as genial with her as he had been with Luke. Obediently she answered his questions. Yes, she was on holiday. No, she had nothing to declare.

'Enjoy your 'oliday, *madame*,' he said with a smile that lifted the rather tired lines of his face. He looked as if he was the harassed father of several teenagers, Sally decided; her own father, of course, had been long gone by the time she reached her teenage years. She gave the officer a wide smile. '*Merci beaucoup, m'sieur.*'

With automatic gallantry he sketched a bow. Her spirits lightened, she stepped out on the deck.

The *Miquelon* was moored at a concrete dock that disappeared into the fog before it joined the land. Of the town there was no sign. But on the dock Dunc was waving to her from beside a small taxicab, and Bev was smiling in her direction. She hurried down the gangplank. The driver under his old navy blue beret had a creased face weathered to a rich nut-brown; so the sun must sometimes shine in St Pierre. Sally pulled Raoul's note from her pocket. '*Pension Gérard Poulain, s'il vous plaît*,' she said, and was immensely pleased when the driver nodded casually, taking her French for granted.

'Our *pension* is on Rue Albert Briand,' said Dunc, studying a map. 'Where's yours?'

'It says Rue Boulot.'

'Then I guess we'll be going to ours first.'

The drive through the town was crowded with first impressions: tiny houses marching up the hillside; rows of multicoloured fish shacks; wet-looking flowers in an open square; cafés and old-fashioned shops lining the streets. The *pension* where the Cuthberts were staying was painted bright green, with a vegetable garden planted in neat rows in the dark soil. 'We'll be eating at the Hôtel Ile-de-France this evening,' Dunc said easily, as he levered himself out of the taxi. 'Around seven. Feel free to join us, Sally.'

'That would be nice,' Bev added hospitably. 'Enjoy your day.'

Sally thanked them for the offer without committing herself to it. A short drive brought her to her *pension*, painted mustard-yellow but as clean and tidy as the first one. She paid the driver an assortment of the big colourful notes, rang the doorbell and walked inside. Varnished panelling lined the brown-carpeted hallway; an artificial palm tree with repellently shiny leaves stood in one corner. A woman in a spotless white uniform bustled out of the kitchen. '*Complet, m'mselle, complet!*' she exclaimed in a high-pitched voice.

In careful French Sally explained that she was here to take Raoul Descroches's reservation. The woman fired off a couple of rapid sentences, her hands on her hips. Helplessly Sally said, '*Je ne comprends pas, madame.*' As the sentences were repeated, a little more slowly but equally incomprehensibly, although the word *complet* recurred, Sally only knew with a sinking heart that something was wrong.

A clatter of footsteps came from the stairway at the far end of the hall and a tall girl with a ponytail and an athletic stride came towards her. She took in the situation in a glance and said breezily to Sally, 'Gotta problem?'

After Sally had explained the situation, the girl spoke to the woman in staccato French and an animated conversation ensued. The girl finally turned to Sally. 'Sorry,' she said, 'but you're out of luck. Your friend Raoul was supposed to have sent a deposit to hold the room two weeks ago, and because he didn't Madame Poulain has given it to someone else. It's Bastille Day on Wednesday, you see, so this is the busiest week of the year. You can hardly blame her.'

'Oh,' said Sally blankly. 'Then I'll have to try somewhere else.'

The girl addressed a question to Madame Poulain, who nodded vigorously, spread her hands in a very Gallic expression of resignation, and disappeared into

the kitchen. 'You can leave your bag here if you like,'
the girl explained. 'It'll be perfectly safe. If I were you
I'd go to the tourist bureau down by the post office, and
get a list of all the available places. Good luck!' She
bounced out of the door and ran down the steps.

Sally put her case by the palm tree, inwardly cursing
Raoul for his carelessness, and more slowly followed
the girl down the steps. Her sense of direction had
always been good, and she remembered passing the
post office on the way to the Cuthberts' *pension*. She
had also passed a *pâtisserie*. She set off down the street.

Twenty minutes later, fortified by a cup of very strong
black coffee and two huge buns, she was on her way
again. Three hours later, when she ordered an open-
faced ham sandwich for lunch at a café, she was not
feeling nearly as optimistic. The hotels and *pensions*
were all full, and she was very much afraid if one more
person said to her, with a shrug and upraised palms,
'But *m'mselle*, it is soon Bastille Day, you understand,'
she would start screaming, much as the French
peasants storming the great grey prison had done two
centuries earlier. She had a small list of private boarding
houses. If these were also *complet*, she had no idea what
she was going to do. Throw herself on the mercy of the
local *gendarmerie*? Beg the Cuthberts to let her sleep on
the floor? The one bright spot in the day was that she
had not run into Luke. She had too much pride to want
him to discover her rather foolish predicament.

At two o'clock Sally had gone through her entire list
of addresses without finding a place to stay. Trying to
tamp down panic, she was walking back towards the
town when she saw a printed sign in the window of a
mean little house that was squeezed between two
others on one of the back streets. *Chambre à Louer* the
sign said. A large and lethargic angora cat regarded her
coldly from beneath the sign.

The house was not prepossessing. But Sally was

discouraged enough by a long day of refusals to raise her fist and knock on the door.

The cat yawned, then closed its amber eyes. Sally knocked again, heard a voice from inside call out impatiently, and was rewarded by the door swinging open. The dimly lit hallway did not look very clean. Neither did the man standing at the door. Although a cursory glance would have found him not bad looking, closer inspection revealed a two-day stubble covering his jaw, and bags under his eyes, which were bloodshot and had thick sandy lashes. He was looking at her with an unpleasant combination of suspicion and a leer. *'Madame?'* he said.

She somehow knew he was mocking her, that he had instantly taken note of her ringless fingers, for he was that kind of man. She stumbled out a question about the room to rent.

'Ah, oui. Very nice room. *Exactement* what you want. And for you, very cheap. Enter, *madame*, enter.' Imperiously he waved Sally indoors.

She did not like his looks. But if he was running a boarding house he must have a wife, and she would only be using the room for sleeping. Sally walked inside.

He reached around her to close the door, then with a flourish introduced himself as Christophe Michel Landry. 'Please call me Christophe, *madame*. This way, please, for the room.'

The house smelled musty and she saw no signs of a wife. The room for rent was at the back of the house up a flight of creaky stairs. It was tolerably clean, although Sally knew she would not have the courage to lift the purple-flowered bedspread to check under the bed. She found out the price and decided to take the room; partly because she had very little choice and partly because she did not want to spend any more of her limited time on the island looking for a place to stay. She signed her

name in the scribbler that served as a guest book, paid
for the room in advance when Monsieur Landry made
it clear this was his policy, and told him she would be
back later with her luggage.

Even though the sky was still a dull, uniform grey
and the air wet with fog, Sally was glad to get outdoors
again. She wandered back to the centre of town, where
she spent an enjoyable afternoon poking around the
shops. She found some very sheer black stockings from
Paris for Lynette, and a hockey shirt labelled St Pierre
Cougars for Caleb. Cecilia presented more of a
problem; and Sally was getting hungry again. She had
somehow decided in the course of the afternoon not to
join the Cuthberts for dinner at the hotel, for she felt
more adventurous than that. So she went into a bar by
the waterfront, and when she had ordered a carafe of
wine and the fish speciality, surveyed her
surroundings. To amuse herself she tried to see the
place through Lynette's eyes; in terms of available men,
how would Lynette rate Antoine's Bar?

There were certainly several attractive young men in
the bar. But they were either in noisy groups or else
with equally attractive young women. There was a
heavy-set, grey haired man sitting alone on a stool at
the counter; although clean-shaven, his face sagged like
that of Monsieur Landry, and carefully Sally avoided
catching his eye. There was a group of over-vivacious
girls at the other end of the counter, and two couples
who looked as though they could be cousins of the
Cuthberts seated at the sturdy wooden tables. And that
was all. No handsome and lonely Lotharios waiting to
be rescued, no modern French equivalents of Sir Philip
Sidney wanting to write poetry to the beauty of her
eyes. And then the door opened and the two camera
enthusiasts from the *Miquelon* walked in. They saw
Sally immediately, joined her with loud cries of
enthusiasm, and also ordered the fish speciality.

Inwardly Sally had to laugh. Lynette would not think much of Antoine's Bar.

When Helen suggested after dinner that the three of them walk up to the cemetery, something of a curiosity because the dead were buried above the ground under elaborate stone monuments, Sally was perfectly agreeable, and on the way collected her suitcase from the *pension* and dropped it off at Monsieur Landry's. The two ladies were rather doubtful about her choice of a place to stay. 'Is it clean, dear?' asked Bertha. 'I'd lock your door at night,' suggested Helen more forthrightly.

'I will, I promise,' said Sally, amused and rather touched by their concern.

The cemetery, enveloped in mist, had a macabre fascination because of its white-painted tombs and gaudy plastic flowers, its photographs of the dead and its prayers for their repose. In bizarre contrast, the three women dropped into one of St Pierre's several nightclubs on the way back to town. Toe-tapping music came from a band of four moustachioed men on a tiny platform, while the dancers on the smooth hardwood floor were by no means confined to the young; several of the couples doing an impeccable fox-trot to the music would never see fifty again. The bar was in steady use.

Five minutes after they had seated themselves at a little corner table Sally was asked to dance. One of her more overt rebellions against her mother had been to take dancing lessons at junior high in her lunch-hour, and although her opportunities to use these lessons had been limited, she soon discovered she had not forgotten them. The atmosphere of the club was such that husbands of some of the couples asked her to dance, and soon Bertha and Helen were on the floor, too. Then Sally was passed from one to the next of a group of Newfoundlanders over from St John's for Bastille Day. Although they had been made loquacious by the rum which they drank as if it were water, their agility was in no way impaired, and when the band played a couple of square sets they took over the dance-floor, whooping at the tops of their lungs, swinging their partners with gusto. Somehow they all reminded Sally of Caleb, but she was having a marvellous time and that was enough.

By one o'clock the rum was getting the better of the Newfoundlanders, so Sally, Bertha and Helen left the club, walking down the quiet streets to Sally's room. The cat was still stationed in the window, which was faintly lit. 'I wish we had an extra bed in our room,' Helen said.

'So do I, dear,' responded Bertha.

At one o'clock in the morning the house looked considerably more sinister than it had in daylight. Said Sally valiantly, 'I'll only be in it for a few hours each night . . . thanks, both of you. I had a wonderful time.'

Bertha giggled. 'I haven't had so much fun in twenty years.'

Helen gave her friend a look of affectionate resignation. 'That means we'll be going back there tomorrow. Or rather today. Join us, Sally, if you'd care to. And now we'd better head home.'

Sally watched them walk away, Bertha prancing a little as if the music were still playing in her head; she also wished there were an extra mattress they could put on the floor of their room. Then, mentally girding herself, she opened the front door of Monsieur Landry's boarding house.

It was wrapped in silence. She sneaked past the parlour door, ascertaining that the cat was the parlour's only occupant. She crept up the stairs, her progress far from quiet because nearly all the steps creaked. Then she started down the hallway along a strip of worn flowered carpeting. A voice spoke in her ear. 'You have the good time tonight, *madame*?'

Sally jumped, almost dropping her bag, and swung

around in the direction of the voice. It belonged, of
course to Monsieur Christophe Michel Landry, who
was lounging against the doorway of what must be his
bedroom, for she could see a crumpled double bed in
the dim glow of a tasselled bedside lamp. He was
wearing tight-fitting trousers and nothing else, seemed
both younger and larger than she remembered, and
smelled strongly of cheap wine.

Lynette's blithe description of amorous Frenchmen
did not seem to apply. Sally clutched her handbag to
her breast and said steadily, 'Thank you, yes, I had a
very good time. Goodnight.'

But he took her by the elbow, his fingers
unexpectedly strong. 'I also can show you the good
time,' he said, and displayed his teeth in a suggestive
smirk. They looked like false teeth.

Had the circumstances been otherwise Sally could
have laughed him off, because his whole manner
reeked of third-rate farce. But she was almost sure that
he and she were the only people in the house; and she
was also aware that she had nowhere else to go.

Although in the course of her upbringing she had
consciously refused to adopt many of her mother's
attitudes, she had inherited one quality from Ruth
Dexter, something her mother would have called
backbone; Ruth did not like people who whimpered in
the hands of fate. So now Sally straightened to her full
height, her grey eyes hard as stone, and said coldly,
'Please let go, Monsieur Landry.'

'Ah . . . you have spirit. Most English girls are so
dull.'

She did not think this was the time to give him a
feminist lecture on his use of the word girl. 'I wish to go
to my room,' she said in a clipped voice. 'Kindly release
me.'

If anything his hand tightened its grip. Sally knew
that if he tried to haul her into his bedroom she would

begin to scream regardless of whether there were anyone to hear her; and when he said, '*Eh bien* . . . just one little kiss first,' she felt panic tighten her throat. If she never kissed another man in her whole life she would not kiss Monsieur Landry now.

But he was strong; and quite possibly thought she was merely being coy. The smell of wine grew stronger as he bent his head to hers.

Caleb had taken lessons in self-defence rather than dancing in junior high, and had practised some of his skills on his sister. So now Sally went limp, lashed out with her free hand and one foot, and had the satisfaction of hearing Monsieur Landry give a very unromantic grunt. He let go of her arm, gasping for air.

'If you come near me again I shall call the police,' she said in a frigid voice. 'Goodnight.' And she marched down the hall to her own room.

Once inside she closed the door, saw that it lacked a lock or bolt, and hauled a heavy black desk in front of it, not caring how much noise she made. She then discovered that she was shaking. She sat down on the bed, clasping her hands together to keep them still, and wished it were morning.

But it was not even one thirty. Eventually Sally took off her shoes and lay down on the bed, fully dressed, pulling her rain-jacket and sweater over her. The house was completely silent. She closed her eyes, knowing she would never sleep, and when she opened them felt the warmth of sunlight falling across her face from the window at the back of the house. Sunlight . . . it must be morning.

She scrambled off the bed and hurried to the window, parting the frayed net curtains to look over the back of the nearest house and Monsieur Landry's unkempt garden. But the grass was a vivid green on the rocky hillside behind the town and the sky a clear, unclouded blue, so that even though the curtains smelled of stale smoke and Monsieur Landry remained a problem, Sally found that she was smiling.

She changed into a brightly flowered shirt and washed at the basin in her room. Then she closed her case, moved the desk away from the door and used the bathroom across the hall. Monsieur Landry's door remained shut. But when Sally went downstairs there was a sheet of white paper on the little table by the door, her name prominently printed across the top. Underneath was written, 'Your room occupied tonight. You leave by 10.00 hours. C.M. Landry, prop.'

Slowly Sally put the paper back on the table. She was not surprised that he had chosen to communicate by letter rather than in person, for she had damaged his pride last night far more than his shins. Nor was she sorry to be seeing the last of his house. What upset her was that she had nowhere else to go.

She went back upstairs and got her case, hurrying to be gone before the other bedroom door should open. The angora cat was squatting by the door. It neither rubbed against her legs nor mewed a welcome: simply waited, cold-eyed, until she opened the door, and then bolted through. Sally pulled the door shut and set off down the street. Breakfast first, she decided, remembering the *pâtisserie*. Then she would plan a course of action.

Several other people had had the same idea as she; all the tables were occupied. As she stood irresolutely in the doorway, the strong scent of coffee tantalising her nostrils, a tall young man with a beard and blond hair, who was sitting alone at a table in front of the window, stood up and beckoned to her. 'Why don't you join me?' he said.

His smile was pleasant and she was very hungry, so she sat down across from him and introduced herself. His name was Noel and he was from New Zealand, a country that had always appealed to her. They fell into an easy conversation, during which Noel demolished four pastries to her two and downed three mugs of coffee. He was booked on a deep-sea fishing trip leaving later that morning, he told her, adding with visible regret, 'I know it's booked up, or I'd suggest you come along. But we'll be back by dark, and I always go to the Select Club in the evenings, have you been there? Great place if you like to dance. And drink,' he added as an afterthought.

'I love to dance,' said Sally.

'Great! Turn up any time after nine thirty, be fun seeing you again.' He reached across the table and shook her hand, as if sealing a pact. Sally smiled back, rather liking him. They talked for a few minutes longer before Noel picked up both bills and pushed back his chair. 'You let me pay for this,' he said firmly. 'It's probably none of my business, but I've been wondering why you're carrying your case— changing *pensions*?'

Sally relayed the story of Raoul and of Monsieur Christophe Michel Landry, trying not to sound too melodramatic. But Noel's blue eyes were on fire with indignation and all his macho instincts aroused. 'I'd have punched him out for you!' he exclaimed, flexing his not inconsiderable muscles.

Sally refrained from telling him that she had managed fine on her own. 'The result is that I have to find another place to stay,' she finished temperately.

But she had aroused other instincts as well. 'You could stay with me,' Noel said. 'I'm in the hotel across from the tourist bureau . . . I'd really like you to stay.'

It was, quite openly, an invitation. Sally said carefully, 'Noel, I'm not into casual relationships.'

He gave her a frank smile. 'I'd behave myself. If that's what you wanted.'

She said, not very cleverly, 'Oh. I see.'

He added with boyish enthusiasm, 'But it'd be fine

with me if you didn't want to behave.'

There was something just a little too ingenuous in his smile. Sally said bluntly, 'Sex is out.'

'You're much too pretty to be making statements like that—and you'll have a hard time finding somewhere else to stay this close to Bastille Day.' His eyes twinkled. 'So you'd better keep me in mind. And now I've got to go or I'll miss the boat. Don't forget, nine thirty. The Select.'

Noel leaned over and kissed her on the cheek, gave the cashier a handful of notes and a big smile, and strode out of the *pâtisserie*. Through the window he blew her another kiss, and because she was both watching him and carrying on an inner dialogue with herself she did not see the dark-haired man who entered the restaurant as Noel left. A voice that could have been Lynette's was whispering insinuatingly into her ear, You might have to stay with him, Sally.

For all his fine talk about behaving himself, I don't trust him.

You don't trust anything in trousers. Right?

I don't want to have an affair!

And then a real voice spoke in Sally's ear, a voice several notes deeper than Lynette's and a great deal angrier. 'It didn't take you long to find yourself a man,' it said.

CHAPTER FIVE

SALLY would have known that voice anywhere. She looked up, aware of a ridiculous and inappropriate surge of happiness, and said with a calmness that she was rather proud of, 'Good morning, Luke.'

Without waiting to be invited Luke sat down in the chair that Noel had occupied. He was wearing a blue and white striped shirt under a V-necked pullover and his eyes were just as blue as she had remembered them. Much bluer than Noel's. 'Didn't you hear what I said?' he snapped.

'Yes. I heard.'

'You must have spent the night with him—why did you send him packing? Didn't he measure up?'

Her nostrils flared. 'I did *not* spend the night with him! Do you always think the worst of everyone? Or is there something special about me?'

He ticked off his fingers with a logic that infuriated her. 'I know that you're looking for a man. I know I declined to be that man. I see you having breakfast with a man who kisses you before he leaves. What the hell am I supposed to think. I'm not totally naïve!'

She decided to carry the war into his zone. 'But you're very upset—why, Luke? After all, *you* don't want an affair with me. So why should you care what I do?'

'Because you don't look like a tramp,' he said shortly.

'That's because I'm not,' she retorted.

'So you just happened to meet that guy half an hour ago and he just happened to kiss you before he left—come off it, Sally. I'm not stupid, either.'

There was genuine bitterness in the line of Luke's mouth. Too much bitterness, Sally thought, feeling her temper die down. She said, attempting to defuse some of his anger, 'Arguing at this hour in the morning makes me hungry. I'm going to get another coffee and one of those deliciously fattening chocolate croissants. Can I get you one as well?'

He looked at her in a baffled silence and quite suddenly Sally knew she would never accept Noel's invitation regardless of how he behaved himself. She did not care if she never saw Noel again. But she did care about Luke's opinion of her. Cared a great deal. And explain that to me, Lynette, she thought wryly.

'A coffee would be OK,' Luke said finally.

They went up to the counter together, where the waitresss, the same black-eyed beauty who had taken the money from Noel, gave Sally a look of considerable respect. After Luke succumbed to a pastry filled with custard and strawberries, they took their coffee back to the table. Sally stirred hers and said, 'Now, let me tell you exactly what I have been doing since I saw you last.'

'The truth, the whole truth and nothing but the truth?'

'Yes! Exactly so.'

'Too bad there's not a Bible handy.'

'Strangely enough I'm in the habit of telling the truth—my mother saw to that. But if you're determined to disbelieve me, Luke, I might as well save my breath. Because basically what I'm going to tell you is what I've been repeating to the point of boredom ever since we met—I'm not looking for a man!' Sally took a big mouthful of the croissant, even in her exasperation relishing the flakiness of the pastry and the smoothness of the chocolate on her palate.

Luke leaned across and brushed her chin with one finger. 'A crumb,' he said.

His touch had sent a tingle along her nerves; and his mouth had relaxed a little. Willing herself not to blush, Sally asked, 'So do we talk about last night or do we talk about the weather?'

'The weather bores me as a topic of conversation.'

She had to smile. 'I promise not to bore you,' she said. She began with her visit to the *pension* where Raoul was to have had a room for her, and continued from there, not sparing him the dearth of available men in the bar or the drunken Newfoundlanders in the club. She had Luke's full attention, she could tell, although she was almost certain he was withholding judgement. When she described the shenanigans of Monsieur Landry at one o'clock in the morning, Luke did not leap from his chair vowing vengeance, as had Noel. He merely said, a small smile on his lips, 'What did you do, Sally?'

'I kicked him in the shins and punched him just below the sternum,' she said. 'Very effective. He let go.'

'I'm sure he did—remind me not to tangle with you. And do go on, this saga is far more entertaining than the weather.'

She finished with a totally accurate account of her breakfast with Noel and his invitation for the night with its various possibilities. And there she stopped, rather abruptly, and took another large bite of the croissant.

'So you accepted, I'm sure,' said Luke smoothly, his eyes trained on her face in a way a number of former convicts would have recognised.

Sally swallowed and wiped her mouth with her serviette. 'I didn't actually.'

'He looked a decent enough fellow to me.'

'Oh, no doubt,' Sally said ironically. 'But what if his scenario is that we share the bed and my scenario is that we don't? He's considerably bigger than me, and not everyone falls for the old kick-in-the-shin routine. Put yourself in my shoes, Luke Sheridan—try and imagine you're female and five feet five . . . it removes quite a few options, believe me.'

Luke's face was inscrutable. 'So where are you going to stay tonight?'

Sally bit into the croissant again, thinking that her indecisiveness was very likely to make her fat. 'The park bench?' she hazarded.

'You can stay with me. At my hotel.'

Sally choked on a crumb. Luke patted her back with rather overdone solicitude and waited until she had gulped down some coffee. 'Did you hear me?'

'Why do you think I choked?'

'You mean the prospect nauseates you?'

Sally let out her breath in an exaggerated sigh. 'You have a gift for twisting my motives!'

'I certainly lack the gift for understanding you.' His smile was both sardonic and self-deprecating. 'At my job I'm known for my discernment—I must have left it behind when I came on board the boat. Because I would have sworn you were out for an affair.'

She looked him full in the eye. 'Do you believe me now, Luke?' she asked, and felt her hands clench in her lap; she desperately wanted him to believe her.

Although he hesitated, he did not drop his eyes. 'I'm beginning to,' he said slowly.

It was by no means a whole-hearted endorsement. 'You trust me about as much as I trust Noel,' Sally said.

Luke leaned back in his chair; Ross Deighton, who knew him well, would have known he was not nearly as relaxed as he looked. 'So which of us is it to be?' he said. 'Me or Noel? A simple choice.'

'You've got it wrong,' Sally said calmly. 'The choice is between you and the park bench.'

Something flickered behind Luke's eyes. 'Noel's out of the running, is he? What's so special about me, Sally?'

The most difficult question he could have asked. Fumbling for the truth, she said, 'I have the feeling I can trust you—don't ask me why.' Her smile was twisted. 'You also made it abundantly clear that you don't want an affair with me—so in my eyes you're safe. If we were to share a room, I'd figure you'd keep your distance. Unlike Noel.'

Luke raised a derisive eyebrow. 'I'm only human, Sally Cowan. You can share my room on one condition—that you'll wear one of my shirts over that skimpy nightgown of yours.'

Sally said evenly, 'My friend Lynette wanted me to find a lustful Frenchman on this trip. So she substituted that rather obscene remnant of pink satin for my regular nightgown. Which is one even Monsieur Landry would have problems with.'

'How very interesting,' Luck said blandly. 'You raise any number of interesting questions.'

'None of which I shall answer. I just don't like being called a tramp.'

An unwilling smile pulled at Luke's mouth. 'I shouldn't have said that about you, Sally. I don't think it's true.' He glanced at his watch. 'So which is it to be—the Hôtel Philippe or the park bench?'

Sally stared at him wordlessly, her fingers gripping the edge of the table so tightly that her nails were white at the edges. The moment of decision. It was not the moment to remember the aching sweetness of Luke's fingers on her breast or her mindless surrender to his kiss. Was she a fool to trust him? Could she even trust herself? She blurted, 'You mustn't kiss me again.'

'You said you trusted me, Sally.'

'You did kiss me in the cabin. And I'm sure if I tried to kick you, your shin would be somewhere else.'

'I believe it would. So you haven't forgotten that kiss.'

'Had you?'

'Oh, no,' he said smoothly. 'I hadn't forgotten it.'

Under her flowered shirt Sally's breasts rose and fell in tiny, agitated breaths; she could not possibly have been faking the anguish and uncertainty, even in his eyes. 'Can I trust you, Luke?' she begged. 'Please tell me the truth.'

He dropped his sardonic manner. 'Yes,' he said. 'If we share a room, Sally, I won't as much as lay a finger on you.'

She mustered all the backbone her mother had bequeathed her. 'Then I'll stay with you,' she gasped.

'You look as though you're choosing the guillotine,' Luke said harshly.

Sally let go of the edge of the table and sat back in her chair, feeling the intense relief that can follow a major decision. She drank the last mouthful of her coffee, which was cold, and said with gentle mockery, 'Surely not?'

Luke had to smile. She wondered if she was crazy to imagine that it had been a long time since he had been with a woman who made him smile, and heard him say as briskly and impersonally as if they had indeed just finished a discussion of the weather, 'OK, that's settled. We'll take your bag down to the hotel first. Then at eleven I'm meeting a young couple from New Brunswick that I got to know yesterday, we're planning to rent bikes and take a picnic lunch. You'd like to join us, wouldn't you?'

Sally would have agreed to any plan that would prevent her and Luke spending the day in the hotel room. 'That sounds like fun—they won't mind a fourth person?'

'Not at all. Their names are Carol and Mike, you'll like them. I said I'd look after getting the food, and they'll make the arrangements for the bicycles—so we'd better go.'

As naturally as if he were her husband he bent and

picked up her suitcase. And Sally, independent Sally, said not a word, following him out of the *pâtisserie* as obediently as a feudal wife. She felt as though she was moving in a dream, as if the jostling tourists, the old-fashioned shops, the self-important, honking cars were all unreal, and would fade away if she reached out to touch them. Only Luke was real. Luke, in whom she was placing her trust.

They walked downhill towards the harbour, which sparkled in the sun. The Hôtel Philippe was small and charming, with an iron gate and walls of pink stucco; a tangle of petunias edged its walk. Nor was it anywhere near the tourist bureau, Sally saw with relief; she would not want to stay in the same hotel as Noel. Luke marched straight to the front desk and held a low-voiced conversation with the clerk in very rapid French. He wrote something in the guest-book, passed over some money and then turned back to Sally. 'One flight up,' he said. 'Here's a key for you.'

The metal was cold against her fingers. Without saying a word she trotted up the stairs behind him. There was a palm tree on the landing that reminded her, sharply, of the *pension* where she should have been staying. Then Luke was unlocking the door to his room. Their room, thought Sally, wondering what in the world she was doing there.

It was a pleasant room, very much cleaner than Monsieur Landry's, and filled with sunlight. But Sally came to a dead stop just inside the door. In the middle of the room, headboard against the wall, was the bed. A double bed. Meant for two.

Bedrooms by their very nature contain beds. But had Sally not heard Luke shut the door behind her, she would probably have turned and run. 'I—I thought there'd be twin beds,' she stammered.

He had followed the direction of her gaze. 'Well, there aren't. Obviously.'

'You should have told me!'

'You really are paranoid, aren't you? You're registered now, Sally—the decision's made.'

Sally had grown to hate the double bed that she and Bruce had shared, for it had become a symbol of all that was wrong with their marriage. 'Then one of us will have to sleep on the floor,' she said stubbornly.

'It won't be me. I told you you could trust me, and I meant it.'

She tried to force her brain into action. 'I owe you some money. For the room.'

'We'll settle up when we leave.'

'I didn't realise you'd have to give my name.'

'Hotels frown on men who have women in their rooms without paying for double occupancy.'

The words were out before she thought. 'So you've done this before?'

'That's not what I said,' Luke lashed back. But something in her pinched face must have touched him, because he added more gently, 'We have a real luxury—a private bathroom. Why don't you put your swimsuit on under your clothes, because we thought we'd try and find a beach. Then let's go shopping.'

So they were not going to linger in the room. Sally gave Luke a smile in which relief was a major component, grabbed her case and vanished into the bathroom. It was minuscule. But it afforded her much-needed privacy, and for that she was grateful.

Her swimsuit was a striped bikini, a birthday gift from Lynette; she put shorts on over it, looping a long-sleeved sweater around her neck over her shirt, and carrying a towel and her sunhat went back in the bedroom. Luke took the towel from her and put it in his haversack. He too was wearing shorts. He had, she thought with a little shiver of apprehension, beautiful legs. She was not sure he had even noticed hers.

They left the hotel and climbed back up the hill,

buying wine in one shop, smoked trout, fruit and
cheese in another, long sticks of bread and pastries in a
third. The bicycles were clustered on a street corner,
where Carol, a pretty brunette, and Mike, a rangy
redhead, were already waiting for Luke. Both seemed
genuinely pleased to add Sally to their outing and
quickly arranged for a fourth bicycle.

The shopping expedition, so very ordinary, had
relaxed Sally; and Luke was not going to fall on her in
front of Carol and Mike. She began to enjoy herself.
They cycled through town, climbing a great many hills,
until they came to Rue Savoyard, which eventually
sloped downwards past hills scraped bare of
vegetation, past summer cottages and fields full of
wildflowers. A piebald horse jogged along the fence as
they passed, and birds sang in the bushes. They took a
dirt road labelled *plage*, arriving at a pebbled beach
where waves lapped on the shore in peaceful rhythm.
Leaving the bicycles by the bank, they tramped down to
the seaweed-covered rocks and spread their towels on
the sand. 'A swim,' said Carol decisively. 'We can't go
to St Pierre and not have a swim.'

Her husband stepped out of his deck shoes, stuck his
toe in the water and hurriedly withdrew it. 'You might
change your mind,' he said.

Carol grinned at him, stripping off her shorts and top.
'It'll give you an appetite.'

'We're not going to let them outdo us, are we?' Luke
said to Sally.

She had, wincingly, tested the water as well. 'I don't
feel at all competitive.'

He laughed. 'If you don't get wet, you don't get an
éclair.'

'Tyrant,' she said primly.

He unbuttoned his shirt and stepped out of his
shorts. Sally's eyes slewed away from him. She turned
her back and took off her own clothes, dropping them

on the towel. Then, prepared to do anything rather than look at Luke again, she followed Carol's example and ran into the water.

It was so cold that it drove from her mind the image of Luke's long, muscular body in its brief blue trunks. Carol was shrieking as loudly as she. The two men joined them and all four played a noisy and vigorous game of water tag, for ordinary swimming seemed out of the question. Then with one accord they all ran for the shore.

'Thank goodness that's over,' Mike said, towelling the red spikes of his hair. 'Now can we eat?'

Sally's flesh was covered with goose bumps. But the sun was hot and the sand was warm and she had never tasted anything as delicious as smoked trout on crusty French bread. She gave Luke an uncomplicated smile of pleasure, licking her fingers, and heard Carol say, 'Where are you from, Sally?'

Without consciously having thought about it, Sally knew she did not want to reveal much of her personal background, for Cecilia and Caleb and all the struggles of the past years seemed to have no place in the strange relationship between her and Luke. She said, 'I live in Sydney.'

'Steel capital of the east,' Mike joked; the steel plant in Sydney was perennially in the red.

'I've never been to Sydney,' Carol replied. 'But a school friend of mine lives there, Petra MacLean, do you know her?'

'Sydney's full of MacLeans and MacDonalds,' Sally said, relieved that Carol did not know the city, for she herself had only been there once.

'What do you do?' This from Mike, although Sally was aware that Luke was listening to every word she said.

She told the truth. 'I run my own secretarial service—typing and word-processing for businesses and college people.' Rather heavy-handedly she tried to change the subject. 'Let's not talk about work, this is my first holiday in ages!'

Carol began a very amusing description of their last holiday, a package tour to the West Indies that had been less than well organised, and Sally relaxed. Telling lies was not her forte, she decided, and she was unfortunately made even more aware of this half an hour later when the last of the wine had disappeared and they were all stretched out on their towels in the sun. Luke was lying next to Sally, Carol and Mike a little apart from them. Said Luke, 'Whereabouts in Sydney do you live, Sally?'

She searched her memory. 'Prince Street.'

'Near the shopping centre?'

'Further out. I have an apartment in an older house.' That would be appropriate for a glorified secretary, wouldn't it?

'I get up to Sydney once or twice a year on business. I'll have to get your phone number and address.'

Inwardly horrified, for it was one thing to say she was from a certain city, another to be expected to produce a phone number, Sally managed what she hoped was a non-committal smile and said casually, 'That would be nice.'

She did not feel casual. She was not at all sure why she had lied to him, this dark-haired man who angered and attracted her in equal measure. Because she was frightened by the strength of that attraction? She sneaked a glance at the supple flow of muscle under his tanned skin and the tangled hair on his deep chest and admitted to herself with an inward tremor that Luke was the first man in five years to attract her sexually. Certainly he was as different from Dennis as night from day.

He had said she could trust him. But she had caught him watching her once or twice during the picnic, his

eyes on the swell of her breasts as she leaned forward to
help herself to grapes or on the slim line of her thighs
on the beach towel; and each time she had remembered
the way he had touched her in the cabin. As if he had
wanted her and hated her at the same time, she
thought uneasily.

Yet she had seen another side to him today as he had
fooled around in the sea and messily apportioned an
over-ripe Camembert: a carefree side, friendly and fun-
loving, that made him seem younger and much less
formidable. She had liked that side of him, she thought,
closing her eyes against the sun's glare on the sand.
She was silly to worry. Of course she could trust him.

A tiny smile on her lips, she dozed off.

The rest of the day followed easily and without strain.
Later in the afternoon the four of them bicycled further
along the coast and sighted seals stretched out on the
rocks and bobbing in the water. On the way back into
town they came across a practice session of *pelote basque*,
a violent game of ball played against a cement wall, and
watched it for almost an hour before returning the
bicycles. They agreed to meet at seven for dinner. This
time climbing the stairs to the hotel room seemed quite
natural to Sally. She took off her sneakers inside the
door and said impishly, 'Me first in the bathroom—it'll
take me longer to make myself beautiful.'

Luke looked from her salt-stained feet to her tousled
red curls. 'You've already achieved your aim.'

The warmth of the sun seemed to linger in his eyes,
holding all the magic of the day they had spent
together. Sally said impulsively, 'I enjoyed your
company today, Luke.'

'And I yours.' His smile was unguarded. 'Off you go,
we've only got an hour to get ready.'

Because of the demands of Cecilia and Caleb, Sally
was used to quick changes; she was showered and

dressed in thirty-five minutes. She hesitated briefly before opening the door and stepping back into the bedroom, because Luke had not seen her in a dress before. Her haltered sundress, which was splashed with green and red and white, had been on sale in one of the Halifax malls, and she had been lucky enough to find bright green sandals to match; Lynette had lent her a lacy white shawl for the trip.

But Luke was stretched out on the bed, asleep, his shirt undone so that the scar over his ribs stood out lividly against his tan. Sally said loudly, 'Luke, the bathroom's free.'

His eyes flew open; he was instantly and fully awake in a way that made her slightly apprehensive, although she could not have said why. Leaning on one elbow, he said matter-of-factly, 'I had thought you couldn't possibly be more beautiful than you were at the beach. But I was wrong.'

Over and over again Bruce had damaged Sally's sense of self-worth as a woman; in a few simple words Luke was restoring her pride. 'Thank you,' she murmured, then added, 'Luke, how did you get that scar? And the one on your arm?'

'I'm a parole officer, based at the penitentiary in New Brunswick. This one,' he indicated the white slash on his arm, 'I got trying to break up a fight. The other was was due to a hostage-taking.'

Somehow she was not surprised, for she had sensed a certain toughness in Luke from the beginning, recognising that he was possessed of a strength that was more than physical. She said lightly, 'I'd better behave myself.'

He stood up, smiling at her. 'Like you, I'm on holiday.'

His smile had a most peculiar effect on her knees, so much so that she was glad when he disappeared into the bathroom. She sat down by the window that overlooked the harbour, and tried very hard to think about her family in Stellars Cove.

The four of them ate in the dining-room of St Pierre's largest hotel: *moules marinières, saumon à l'oseille, crêpes flambées*, and for Sally at least, altogether too much wine. She felt as though Carol and Mike were her dearest friends, and Luke the handsome prince to her Cinderella.

Nothing would do but that they go dancing after dinner. Sally paid no attention to where they were going. She had tucked her arm through Luke's; she felt at one and the same time like a headstrong young girl and a beautiful woman. Not until they had passed through a dark entrance-way did she see that the club was named Le Select. Noel. Noel was expecting her here this evening. But not, of course, with Luke.

With a rush of bravado she decided she could handle Noel. Nethertheless, she was conscious of relief when, seated at a table against the wall, she gave the room a quick survey and did not sight Noel's blond head. Noel by now had no doubt found someone else, she decided, and forgot about him.

Luke was a wonderful dancer. They jived and polkaed, did the fox-trot and the cha-cha; they waltzed. Sally's body was pliant in his arms, because of course the dance-floor was safe and touch a natural part of dancing. In a trance from which she did not want to be delivered, she was consequently disconcerted when a blond-haired man approached their table and asked her to dance.

'Hello, Noel,' she faltered, and hurriedly introduced him to her companions, trying to ignore Luke's raised eyebrows. 'Sure, I'd like to dance.'

You're becoming an awful liar, she told herself as Noel led her out on the floor. Sedately they began to fox-trot around the room. Noel said succinctly, 'I was late getting here—is the deal off?'

'Yes,' she said in a small voice.

'He's kind of a tough-looking customer. Not sure I'd want to tangle with him. Sure you know what you're doing?' She nodded again, adding another lie to her total for the day. 'Have you only just met him?'

'No. I met him on the boat.'

'I see.' Noel trundled her between two other couples. 'Listen, Sally, I'm at the Hôtel Langlade if you ever need a place to go.'

For the first time since they had started dancing she looked at him full in the face. 'You're a nice man, Noel,' she said. 'Thank you.'

He grimaced. 'Nice, eh?'

While Noel was disappointed by her new plans he was not devastated. She said demurely. 'Over in the corner by the band there's a table of very pretty young women. I think you should ask one of them to dance.'

'I can take a hint,' Noel replied, grinning down at her. 'You want to go back to that guy.'

'Yes,' Sally said, with an air of discovery. 'Yes, I do.'

'I'm nothing if not obliging,' said Noel, steering her straight across the dance-floor to the detriment of her feet. He pulled out her chair, and with a little bow in Luke's direction said, 'She's all yours.' Then he began walking in a purposeful way towards the table near the band.

'So what was all that about?' asked Luke.

'He was just checking,' Sally said airily. 'Shall we dance?'

'By all means,' Luke replied. The fox-trot had been replaced by another waltz. He led her into the thick of the dancers, where the floor was the most dimly lit, pulled her against the length of his body, and, his feet still moving in rhythm with the music, rested his cheek on her hair.

Sally forgot Carol and Mike and Noel, forgot the music and the other dancers and all her fears. There

was only Luke, the warmth of his embrace and the
strength of his arms. She had no idea how long they
clung to each other in the middle of the dance-floor; but
when the band changed to a jive, Luke abruptly
released her. 'I think we'd better go back to the hotel,'
he said.

Sally blinked, suddenly aware that she had drunk too
much and that the air was full of cigarette smoke.
Another waltz like that, she thought sickly, and she'd
be the one kissing him.

Luke led her back to the table, where Mike was about
to order another round of drinks. 'None for us,' Luke
said easily. 'I think we're going to pack it in.'

Sally hugged Carol and Mike and then she and Luke
left the night club. While they had been dancing the fog
had moved back in, obscuring the stars, blurring the
outlines of the houses, making of a white cat skulking
in an alley a ghostly creature of the night. Sally clutched
her shawl, wishing she and Luke could have been
miraculously transported from their embrace on the
dance-floor to sleep, with no transition in between. The
cool, damp air was sobering, bringing her back to the
reality she had successfully ignored for most of the day:
she was about to share a hotel room with a man who
was a virtual stranger, yet who attracted her as a flame
does a moth. She shivered a little. Luke, whose arm
was around her, stopped, took off his jacket, and put it
over her shoulders. 'Better?' he said.

It was a very ordinary gesture. No reason for her to
feel like bursting into tears. She huddled into the
warmth of the jacket and said, 'Won't you get cold?'

'I'm tough,' he joked.

Sally was sure he was, a thought which did not add
to her composure. They fell silent, listening to the ring
of their steps on the pavement and the echo of music
from another bar. Some people were singing on the
street corner, a melancholy folk-song in a minor key; a

foghorn sounded from the harbour.

With all her heart Sally suddenly wished she were back in Stellars Cove in her bedroom under the eaves, Cecilia asleep in the next room, Caleb across the hall. *That* was her world. Not this one.

CHAPTER SIX

THE desk clerk at the hotel did not even turn around as Luke and Sally came in. After Luke had taken out his key and unlocked the door of their room, Sally handed him back his jacket, which he hung in the cupboard. She took off her shoes, realising for the first time that evening that her feet were hurting. Then she and Luke looked at each other across the room. All the laughter and the ease had gone from his face. Restlessly he moved his shoulders. 'I'm going to have a shower,' he said. 'Won't be long.'

The bathroom door closed. Sally picked up her sandals, placing them neatly in the cupboard, and hung Lynette's shawl over one of the hangers. Then she got her toilet articles and the apricot nightdress from the drawer—the nightdress that Luke had said would not disgrace a prostitute. Absently her fingers smoothed the satin fabric. She must borrow a shirt from him; hopefully it would cover her from neck to knee.

She was still clutching the nightdress when Luke emerged from the bathroom in a cloud of steam, one of the hotel towels wrapped around his hips, his hair curling wetly. She looked the other way. 'You were going to lend me a shirt,' she said loudly.

'Hanging in the cupboard. Help yourself.'

Sally grabbed the largest one and hurried past him, closing the bathroom door firmly behind her. But a shower can only take so long. A few minutes later she was dried, powdered and clad in Luke's shirt. The sleeves hangled over her wrists, the shoulders drooped, and the hem came to mid-thigh. She did not, she thought with relief, look at all provocative. Not giving herself time to think, because if she did she would probably stay locked in the bathroom all night, she opened the door.

Luke was already in bed, the blankets pulled up to his waist. His chest was bare. Not fair, Sally thought crossly. If I'm supposed to be covered up, so should you be. She hung her sundress in the cupboard, then hesitated irresolutely.

'Which is it to be!' Luke said sardonically. 'The bed or the floor?'

Sally glowered at him. 'You're not making this any easier, you know.'

'Was it the Quakers or the Puritans who used to put a board down the middle of the bed?'

With as much dignity as she could muster in the over-sized shirt Sally said, 'There's an extra quilt in the cupboard and I'll take a pillow—I'm going to sleep on the floor.'

He shrugged. 'It's your funeral.'

She had never realised a shrug could be so sexy. She stalked over to the cupboard, pulled out the quilt, which was fortunately a puffy one, and spread it on the floor as far from the bed as she could. She had been a fool to compare him to a prince, she thought stormily; he did not have a chivalrous bone in his body.

She did not want to think about his body. She marched back to the bed, averting her eyes from its occupant, and grabbed the nearest pillow.

'Goodnight, Sally,' Luke said amicably. 'Sweet dreams.'

She gave him a dirty look. 'You're enjoying this, aren't you?'

'I'm starting to realise you really don't want an affair—anyone who'd sleep on a quilt on the floor when there's a perfectly good bed available has the courage of her convictions.'

'Oh, shut up!' Sally flared, and she yanked the pillow from the bed and went back to the quilt. She folded it around herself as best she could, bunched up the pillow and laid her head down, closing her eyes.

Luke switched off the light. She heard the bed creak as he settled himself to sleep. With annoying ease his breathing became slow and regular.

Sally was long to remember that night. The floor was uncompromisingly hard and the quilt not nearly puffy enough. She twisted and turned. Cold air seeped in the gaps, chilling her toes and her knees. She slept and dreamed and woke and wriggled some more. And through it all Luke slept like a baby.

At seven in the morning she could stand it no longer. She went to the bathroom, not being particularly quiet about closing the door, and had a shower, more for warmth than for cleanliness. Then she dressed in jeans and her heaviest sweater. When she went back into the bedroom Luke was still in bed, stretching lazily and yawning. 'Did you sleep well?' he asked with exaggerated innocence.

Her eyes were burning in their sockets and her limbs weighted with tiredness. 'Beautifully, thank you,' she said.

'A girl scout from way back, huh?'

'I founded the movement.'

He laughed. 'You know what? I like you, Sally Cowan.'

She fought back an answering smile. 'Do you? Then you can have the floor tonight.'

'I said like, not adore.' He threw back the covers. Fascinated, she watched him climb out of bed and stretch as unselfconsciously as a cat. Then he grinned at her. 'Want to go to Miquelon today? The boat leaves in an hour and a half and we'll be back by dark. The fog is supposed to lift mid-morning, according to the concierge.'

Miquelon, she knew, was one of the other two
islands that made up the French colony. Maybe the boat
would have a bunk where she could catch up on her
sleep. 'Sure,' she said.

It was another magical day, a day of wheeling
seagulls and pale beaches, of porpoises playing in the
waves and eagles soaring round the cliffs. The little
village of Miquelon was charming, and once again Sally
effortlessly enjoyed Luke's company. He kept
scrupulously to his bargain, never touching her or
treating her other than a casual friend. Part of her was
pleased; part, she was honest enough to admit, was
piqued.

There were no bunks on the boat. At nine thirty that
evening when she and Luke got back to the hotel, Sally
was yawning openly. As Luke ushered her into their
room she muttered, 'A shower and bed.'

'No, Sally. A shower and floor.'

She looked at him through her lashes. 'We could toss
a coin to see who gets the bed.'

He took a coin from his pocket, threw it in the air and
clapped it against the back of his hand. 'Call it.'

'Tails.'

He lifted his hand; the head was showing. Sally said
something very rude and stomped to the cupboard to
get the hated quilt.

By one a.m. she had yet to fall asleep, and all her
nerves were jumpy with over-tiredness. She crept to
the bathroom then back to the quilt and heard Luke
mumble, 'Sally, for God's sake share the bed—you'll be
exhausted tomorrow.'

'I'm fine,' she said brightly, and returned to the quilt.
Luke's breathing settled back into its quiet rhythm; the
floor got harder and her feet colder until suddenly she
could bear her discomfort no longer. She tiptoed over to
the bed. Luke was sleeping on the far side, his back to
her. She lifted the blankets, slid underneath them and

curled up as far from him as she could.

The mattress was gloriously soft. Sally lay still in the darkness and waited for sleep to claim her. But her feet and hands were ice-cold, far too cold for comfort; and Luke was sound asleep. She eased herself across the bed, snuggled into his bare back and let his body heat slowly relax her. Within five minutes she had fallen asleep.

Sally woke to a thick darkness, to warmth and softness and a haze of sensuality. Luke's hands were stroking her body through the thin fabric of the shirt, caressing her breasts and the curve of her waist and hips, slowly and rhythmically, over and over again. She felt as though she were floating, suspended in time and space, a new creature who had never felt this way in her life before. Utterly entranced, she knew she did not want him to stop.

She made a movement towards him in the bed. As if he had been waiting for her, Luke took her in his arms and sought her mouth. His lips were warm, demanding, and very sure of themselves. Trustingly Sally wrapped her arms around his neck.

But before she was ready she felt the impatient thrust of his tongue and the tug of his hands on her shirt. He wrenched his mouth free and muttered hoarsely, 'Take that damn thing off—I want to feel your body.'

'But Luke, I——'

He was struggling with the shirt buttons. As his knuckles grazed her breasts, one of the buttons tore free with a tiny sound that was somehow shocking. Then he had pulled the shirt away from her shoulders and had flung it to the floor and was kissing her again, his hands roaming her body as if he wanted to discover every inch of it in the shortest time possible.

When he freed his mouth it was to seek the peak of her breast with his tongue and all Sally's fears receded

in the piercing pleasure of his touch. Involuntarily she
arched against him, only wanting him to continue the
slow slide of his tongue against her flesh. But Luke
misinterpreted her, pushing her flat on the mattress,
covering her with his body, kissing her again with
brutal strength.

Accustomed to the darkness, Sally's wide-held eyes
could see the black-shadowed bulk of his body, so
much larger than hers, so much more powerful. She
did not think he meant to hold her captive, yet his
weight, the fury of his kiss, the sinewy, ever-seeking
hands all contrived to do so. She felt helpless and
horribly vulnerable, and the delicious haze of sensuality
had retreated.

She had spent a lot of time with Luke the last few
days and would have said she was beginning to know
him. But she had not learned enough, she thought with
a sickening lurch of fear as his thighs forced hers apart.
She should have heeded the bitterness and cynicism
she had seen him display, for they had not been fleeting
emotions: they had represented the real man. For like
Bruce, Luke was making love without tenderness or
patience. She shoved at his chest with the palms of her
hands, trying to wriggle from under him, and gasped
furiously, 'Luke, don't——'

'When you move like that, you drive me crazy,' Luke
muttered thickly, his fingers digging into the soft flesh
of her hips with punishing strength even as his mouth
found her breast again, so briefly that it was like a dart
of flame in the midst of a thunderstorm.

She wanted to cry, 'Please do that again.' But all she
managed was, 'Please——'

'Yes—now,' Luke said fiercely. 'Now.'

When he entered her, Sally felt again that lick of fire.
But the fire was vanquished by a flood of other
emotions: resistance and fear and guilt, so that while
her body was instinctively in rhythm with his, her spirit

was drowning in a vast and terrible loneliness.

She did not have long to wait. His body convulsed. She heard him cry out, a nameless syllable so full of a passionate anguish that the hairs were raised on the back of her neck. She was barred from sharing that anguish, shut out by her lack of response, confirmed by her inadequacies. She felt the deep, inward throb as he found his release, then the frantic racing of his heart against her breast, the pantings of his breath stirring her hair, and wondered if she would ever feel whole again.

He had collapsed on top of her so that she was almost suffocated by his weight. But she held herself very still, and was rewarded when a few moments later Luke threw himself off her to lie flat on his back on his side of the bed. Gradually his breathing slowed to normal, until she became aware with a shock of surprise that he had fallen asleep.

He had not once called her by name. He had not held her with tenderness or given thought to her pleasure. Tears crowded Sally's eyes and trickled down her cheeks, plopping on to the pillow. Staring up into the darkness, she held herself rigidly, terrified of awakening him; she did not think she could bear to have him touch her again.

Time passed; an hour, perhaps. Luke was deeply asleep, and eventually Sally eased herself off the bed. picking up the quilt from the floor, she wrapped herself in it, curled up in one of the chairs and closed her eyes.

She slept fitfully, her nerves on edge, her neck cramped. But time passed, as it must, until through a chink in the curtains the strip of black became the dull grey of dawn. Luke was still asleep, still lying on his back. Envying him for his ability to lose himself so completely, hating him for it at the same time, Sally slid off the chair and crept to the bureau where her track-suit was neatly folded in the drawer. She dressed quickly, laced her sneakers and took her jacket from the cupboard, all the while sneaking glances at the man prone on the bed, and finally picked up her key from the ashtray by the bed.

Luke flung out his arm and muttered something under his breath. Sally shrank to stillness, scarcely breathing, then with immeasurable relief saw him sink back into sleep again. On her tiptoes she edged towards the door, which opened and closed with such a discreet lack of noise that she was both grateful and amused: the first touch of humour she had felt since the night before. The corridor and the stairs were deserted; a uniformed young man was dozing at the counter in the lobby. She pushed open the main door and escaped into the greyness of early morning. Walking very fast, she headed towards the harbour.

The air was cool and moist and the exercise felt wonderful after the night she had spent scrunched in the chair. She walked past the stone figure of a sailor in oilskins staring sightlessly out to sea from the square, and got her sneakers wet in the grass as she tramped along the water's edge where a row of cannons pointed impotently across the harbour. She slanted out along the concrete surface of a quay, the mist closing in behind her so that she was isolated from the land, marooned in a world of rocks and lank brown seaweed where the water sucked and splashed. Dimly through the fog she could see Ile aux Marins, a once-thriving fishing village, now deserted, its weathered buildings dissolving into the mist, its low white church empty of worshippers. Propping herself against the base of the red and white lighthouse at the end of the quay, Sally sat down.

She felt very unhappy. Luke, whom she had begun to like, to whom she had been strongly attracted, was not as he had seemed; he was, instead, exactly like Bruce. How naïve Lynette had been to assume that an affair would solve all Sally's problems, giving her an appreciation of her own sexuality, even a sense of her power as a woman! How wrong! Luke had used her just as Bruce had, his legacy to her an excruciating loneliness and the conviction of failure.

She frowned into the mist. She should never have climbed into bed and curled up to Luke; had she remained on the floor nothing would have happened. Thus far, the fault was hers. But was the fault for her lack of pleasure hers as well? Did she lack something that other women took for granted, some mysterious alchemy that made a man into the lover extolled in romantic movies and fiction, the man of generosity who cared only for his partner's pleasure? Or was this man indeed a product of fiction? Unreal. Non-existent. A creature conjured up by the wishes of women like herself.

At the age of seventeen she had rebelled against the constraints of her upbringing and made love to Bruce, a rebellion that had left her pregnant and forced her into a loveless marriage. In the middle of the night she had made love again, and while pregnancy and marriage were both out of the question this time, the emotional results were the same. A lessening of her self-confidence. An insidious invasion into her consciousness of that horrible word frigid.

A seagull flew by, so close that Sally could hear the wind in its feathers. She wondered where it was going and envied it its freedom. It could leave St Pierre whenever it wanted to . . . if only she could do the same. But her return trip on the *Miquelon* was not scheduled for another five days.

Maybe she could fly. Get on a plane at the little airport across the harbour and go home to Halifax; there were daily flights, she knew. Not until the thought popped into her head did she realise how strongly she wanted to get off the island and away from Luke. She never wanted to see him again; and inwardly congratulated herself that she had lied about her home town. Once she left St Pierre he would never be able to trace her . . . all she had to do was get away. With an optimism born of desperation she decided the fog was bound to lift today just as it had yesterday. And very few people would be leaving the day before Bastille Day, she would be assured of a seat.

Checking her watch, she realised she had two or three hours to wait before the travel agency would be open. But the decision she had made had lifted the burden of depression and failure from her shoulders. So she was no good in bed. So what? She had Cecilia and she had Caleb and she had good friends like Lynette. The world would not come to an end just because she had had a brief, abortive affair. And just thinking of Cecilia made her realise how much she missed her red-haired daughter. It would be wonderful to surprise her and Caleb by walking in the door this evening. It would even be nice to see Sidney.

Getting up from the concrete, which had become increasingly hard while she was sitting there, she strode down the length of the quay and turned right, away from the town. She passed a long row of fishing shacks painted blue, yellow and green, and tidy houses with gardens set among granite rocks; she passed a generating station, its grumbling voice reaching her through the mist long before she saw it; she explored a grotto to the Virgin built half-way up a rocky slope, and picked a bunch of harebells. Then she turned back to the town.

The fog, if anything, was thicker, and Sally felt the first qualm of unease. She did not want to stay in St Pierre. She could not possibly share a room with Luke again. She did not even want to go back to the room to claim her clothes. But her chances of getting anywhere to sleep other than the hotel room were almost nil, for she discovered within herself a strong aversion to throwing herself on Noel's mercies. One man per holiday was enough.

The travel agency was open, its sole occupant a thick-bodied man who looked as if he had a hangover and whose knowledge of English was minimal. Haltingly Sally explained in French that she would like a one-way flight from St Pierre to Halifax.

He gave a snort of laughter and lit a cigarette from the butt of the one smouldering between his fingers. '*Par avion? Non, non!*'

'*Pourquoi pas, m'sieur?*'

'*La brume, madame.*' At her look of incomprehension he added with heavy sarcasm, 'We 'ave a little fog 'ere. No planes.'

'But the fog might lift.' She waved her hands in the air, expressive, she hoped, of fog vanishing into the heavens.

'*Non. Pas aujourd'hui. Demain, peut-être.*' Bored with her, he began sorting through some letters on his desk.

Her disappointment was crushing. Sally turned slowly and walked out of the door, staring at the ground, her hands thrust in the pockets of her track suit.

Someone grabbed her arm. A deep male voice said, 'Thank God I've found you! I've been looking for you everywhere.'

Her head jerked up. It was Luke. The strength of his grip brought back memories Sally could have done without, and in a tiny gesture more telling than words she winced away from him. Briefly he closed his eyes and said in a strained voice, 'Don't look like that, Sally, for God's sake. I can explain.'

But Sally had recovered. With the calmness of extreme rage she said, 'Let go of my arm. There is nothing you can say that I could possibly want to hear.'

His grip tightened. 'You've *got* to listen——'

'Oh, no, I don't!' Her voice rose several notes. 'I

don't even have to *see* you again.'

'You do have to see me,' he said with irritating logic. 'Your luggage is in my room.'

'So it's all of a sudden your room,' she retorted childishly. 'I paid my share, Luke Sheridan. It's my room, too!'

'You'll have to stay there tonight—there's nowhere else for you to go.'

'Don't be so goddamned reasonable!' she spat, and out of the corner of her eye saw a bleary-eyed crowd of men approach the door of the travel agency, among them, she would swear, some of her rum-drinking partners in the club she had gone to with Bertha and Helen. She moved out of their way, but two of them, rather less co-ordinated than they should be, collided with her so that she almost fell against Luke. He let go of her arm, whirled one of the men around and growled, 'Watch where you're going!'

Happily the man was oblivious to any threat. He sent a hazy smile in Luke's general direction, belched, and said, 'Gotta get outa here. Spent all my money. This the right place?'

'Good luck,' said Sally drily.

Reprehensibly she had been gratified by the speed with which Luke had come to her defence, although she had no intentions of telling him so. She said to him coldly, 'Stop taking out your temper on other people, Luke,' and with private amusement watched the men funnel into the travel agency, tripping over each other and swearing with a virtuosity she had to admire.

Luke said tightly, 'Will you kindly pay attention to me?'

She glared at him, the men forgotten. 'Can you give me one good reason why I should?'

The anger left his face. 'I'm not sure that I can, no. I'm doing a lousy job of this, Sally. But please, let's go and find a restaurant and get some breakfast so I can explain what happened last night. Please, Sally.'

He had never begged her for anything before. She paused, searching for the right words. 'Luke,' she said as tactfully as she could, 'I don't think there's much use in your explaining anything. For my own reasons, last night was not a good experience for me, and I really don't want to be in that hotel room with you again. Unfortunately I can't get a flight out of here before tomorrow.' Her smile was rueful. 'It may have to be the park bench.'

He said abruptly, his eyes trained on her face, 'Did you sleep at all last night?'

'Not much, no.'

'I didn't think so—you look tired out. Sally, can we take this step by step? If you'll forgive me for saying so, you also look as though a cup of coffee would do wonders for you, so can we at least have breakfast together? I promise I won't open my mouth if you don't want me to.'

Her resolve never to see him again weakened considerably at the prospect of hot coffee. And he couldn't very well attack her in a restaurant. 'All right,' she said. 'As long as we don't have to walk too far.'

He took her into a poky little restaurant she had not noticed before, where the coffee was piping hot and the croissants as fresh and flaky as any she had ever eaten. Also the chairs were much more comfortable than the concrete quay had been. She cupped her hands around the mug and admitted, 'This was a good idea. I was cold without really realising it.'

'Your hair's damp.'

'Oh, the fire's out all right,' she said, more bitterly than she had intended.

He caught her allusion immediately. 'I put it out, didn't I? Last ight?'

'You didn't help . . . but we agreed we weren't going to talk about last night.'

'Yeah.' Luke sat back in his chair, his blue eyes steady on her face. 'Sally, I think you should go back to the room and have a sleep—you really do look exhausted. I'll stay out all morning and I'll wake you at lunch time. The ferry doesn't leave until this afternoon, anyway.'

She frowned. 'Ferry?'

'There's a daily ferry to Newfoundland, it's not a very long trip. Then you could fly from St John's to Sydney.'

'I didn't know there was one,' she said stupidly.

Luke was trying his best to look after her; and he was telling her obliquely that he would not attempt to keep her here against her will. A sleep would be heavenly, and oddly enough she was sure she could trust Luke to stay out of the room all morning and to wake her in time for the ferry. 'All right,' she said, and saw him try to conceal his relief.

'You've got your key?' She nodded. 'OK. I'll stay here and have another coffee. See you around noon.'

She gave him a small smile and left the restaurant. The thick fog no longer oppressed her, because she could catch the ferry in the afternoon. She went straight to the hotel, went to bed and fell asleep instantly.

CHAPTER SEVEN

SALLY woke at a quarter to twelve, showered and changed into her jeans. She felt refreshed and rested, and her smile when Luke came in through the door was more natural than any she had given him that day. She noticed his quick glance at her suitcase, which she had not yet packed, and knew he had been relieved to find her still in the room. 'Are you hungry?' he asked.

'Starving,' she replied promptly. 'Croissants taste wonderful but an hour later you realise they were mostly air.'

He laughed. 'I'll find you something more substantial than air. Bring a jacket.'

They ate a deliciously thick leek soup, crusty bread and raspberry tarts in the same little restaurant, Sally as always relishing food she had not cooked herself. 'No dishes to wash,' she said contentedly, watching the waitress carry them away. 'I love restaurants.'

'I get the feeling you don't go to them very often.'

'Hardly ever.' Not wanting the conversation to approach her personal life, she asked, 'Do you like to cook, Luke?'

But he was far too astute to be so easily side-tracked. 'What are we going to do, Sally?' he said quietly. 'Am I going to shake your hand and put you on the ferry this afternoon and that's that? Or will you stay and hear me out? I owe you an apology, and I desperately want to try and explain what happened last night.'

'I know what happened,' she said, and could not have prevented the edge in her voice.

He answered hoarsely, 'I swear by all that's holy

that I'll never again do to you what I did last night.'

Sally stared at him in silence, assessing the steadfast sea-blue eyes and the strong lines of his face, then said tentatively, 'It's been a long time since I've felt so lonely as I felt in bed with you last night.'

'I'm sure you were lonely—and with good reason.' He looked around him. 'I don't want to talk about it here, Sally—too many people, and I think it would all come easier if we could be out in the open. By the sea, maybe.'

She said gravely, 'We could rent the bikes again and go back to the beach, and sit on the rocks.'

His hands were gripping his wine-glass so tightly she was afraid he might snap the stem. He said, 'You mean you'll listen?'

'Yes,' she said, and wondered if she was being an utter fool.

He let go of the glass and reached across the table to grasp her hand. 'Thank you, Sally,' he said, and suddenly looked five years younger. 'Come on, let's pay the bill and go and get the bikes.'

The ride to the beach had its own mysterious beauty today, for the fog huddled in the hollows in the fields, and the dampness seemed to accentuate the green of the grass and the yellow of the buttercups. Sally and Luke left the bicycles at the edge of the road and walked down the beach, where the air smelled of salt and wet seaweed. Luke began to gather pieces of driftwood, piling them in a gap between the rocks. Sally followed suit, then perched herself on a rounded boulder as Luke broke up some tiny twigs and touched a match to them. The wood ignited immediately, hissing and spitting. Carefully he fed longer twigs to the flames, his face so intent on his task that she realised with a pang of compassion that he was delaying the explanations he had promised her. She had no idea what he was going to say. Nor could she imagine how any explanation he could make would justify his behaviour of last night. Patiently she waited, holding out her palms to the heat of the fire.

Finally Luke dragged his eyes from the dancing heart of the flames to her face. 'On the way here I tried rehearsing what I was going to say to you. But nothing sounded right. It's funny, I spend a lot of my working life listening to other people's problems, but somehow I seem to have got out of the habit of talking about my own.' He poked another stick into the fire.

Instinctively Sally spoke her mind. 'Do you know what was worst for me last night? You never once called me by name.'

Some of the tension left Luke's face. 'That's because I wasn't making love to *you.*'

Her jaw dropped. 'What on earth do you mean?'

'I had a wife. Her name was—is—Althea. We were divorced a year ago. I hadn't made love to anyone else until I woke in the night and found you there, and in the darkness it was as though you were Althea——'

'But that's horrible!' Unconsciously Sally backed away from him, sitting on her hands on the boulder.

'I'd been so angry with her, Sally. Angry and hurt and frustrated. And I took it out on you.' Through the thin haze of smoke his eyes held hers. 'I'm sorry. More sorry than I can ever say.'

'I don't understand how you could do that!'

'I had no idea that I was going to. I lost control—and you're the one who suffered for it.'

His face was bleak. She somehow sensed he was not expecting her to forgive him but that for the sake of his own integrity he had had to tell her the truth. 'I think you'd better tell me more about her, Luke,' she said.

His gaze dropped to the fire, where the flames were shot through with green and purple from the salt in the driftwood. His voice heavy with memory, he said, 'I met Althea six years ago, just when I'd finished my Master's degree and was starting my first job—heady days. She had hair like a lion's mane and eyes green as a cat's, the most glorious creature I'd ever seen. What was more, she fell in love with me. We married, and for the first couple of years I thought heaven had indeed come to earth. I loved my job, I loved my wife, I had the world by the tail . . .'

Two of the logs collapsed on each other, sending a shower of sparks up into the air. Sally added a couple more chunks of wood. She could picture them together, the cat-like beauty and the rugged, dark-haired man who adored her, and felt a strange pang of what could only be envy. She said quietly, 'What happened, Luke?'

'Euphoria can't last for ever. Sooner or later we had to deal with reality. I wanted a settled life, children, one or two holidays a year. But Althea was in no hurry to have children. She wanted excitement, parties, shopping in Montreal, the theatre in New York. And she hated the demands of my job. When I was offered an administrative position in Ottawa and turned it down, she was furious. But I knew I wasn't ready for administration, that I needed more experience inside the penitentiary dealing with the inmates themselves before I could begin to know what decisions should be made at the management level. So I stuck to my guns. I had to. We muddled along for another couple of years, me giving her as much money as I could for her trips and shopping, going with her whenever possible, giving her the freedom that was so important to her. Because I still loved her—or so I thought—and she could do no real wrong in my eyes. Then I was offered a six-month leave of absence to study the parole system in the United States. We would be based in Boston. Althea was ecstatic. We rented a flat downtown and I submerged myself in the work, travelling all over the States to visit various prisons. Althea didn't always go with me. She preferred Boston and New York.'

Abruptly he stopped. There were deep lines engraved in his face, and Sally knew he had come to the crux of the story. She said evenly, knowing she was right, 'You discovered Althea was having an affair?'

Luke glanced up, his dark head silhouetted against the ever-shifting mist. 'Right. I got home a day early from a trip to Texas and found them together. In our bed. Or what I'd thought was our bed.' With vicious strength he splintered a piece of wood across his knee. 'For the first time in my life I really understood how murders get committed . . . there'd have been a certain irony in that, wouldn't there? Parole Officer Receives Life Sentence. Anyway, I didn't commit murder. The guy left and in the ensuing row I discovered she'd been meeting him in Boston and New York for months.'

Sally said gently, 'I'm beginning to understand why you reacted so strongly when you thought I was looking for an affair. That nightgown caused a lot of trouble, didn't it?'

He paused, head to one side. 'There's such a quality of innocence in you, and yet there you were throwing yourself at me—or so I thought—in that goddamned nightdress. I couldn't handle the situation at all. You don't look the slightest bit like Althea,' he added inconsequentially.

She said delicately, 'There's a saying that all cats are grey in the dark. So last night, even though I don't look the slightest bit like her, I became Althea?'

'Last night was a catharsis,' Luke said heavily. 'I took out on you all my anger against the woman who had made a mockery of my marriage bed. When I first woke up this morning I felt cleansed. Lighter. Free. As though a burden I'd been carrying for a year had been lifted from me. And then, of course, I remembered you. For me it might have been catharsis. But for you—I'd used you. I'd been rough and insensitive, totally selfish.

I didn't blame you for running away. I was only afraid I wouldn't be able to find you and explain. And even now that I've explained I'm aware that there's no real way I can apologise.'

Sally could think of nothing to say. Avoiding his eyes, she prodded the fire with a long stick, watching the charred wood crumble and fall into the coals, which pulsed with a fierce orange glow. She sensed rather than saw Luke get up; every nerve quivering, she heard him walk around the fire to where she was sitting. He knelt beside her, taking the stick from her restless fingers and then capturing her hands in the warmth of his own.

'There is one way I can apologise,' he said in his deep voice. 'I know you're afraid of making love even though I don't know why. But we could go back to the hotel and make love again—and this time I swear would be different. For both of us.'

She pulled her hands free and stood up, clambering round the boulder to put more distance between them. 'Oh, no! No, thanks,' she said incoherently.

Slowly Luke stood up as well. 'I promise I would give you pleasure, Sally.'

A blush scorched her cheeks. 'I don't want to!' she cried.

He stated the obvious. 'You're frightened.'

'After last night, who wouldn't be?' Sally retorted, fully expecting him to snap back at her.

Instead he said calmly, 'So what are your hang-ups, Sally? And why are you so adamant against having an affair?'

By moving away from Luke she had also moved away from the fire. The wind off the sea penetrated her jeans and lifted her damp hair so that she shivered. She shook her head in helpless denial. 'I can't tell you that,' she said.

'I've shared some of my past with you.'

'Yes. But I don't have to do the same.'

'You're cold,' he said abruptly. 'Let's take the bikes back. I'll lend you a sweater and we'll find a nice warm bar.'

Deeply relieved that he had accepted her refusal so easily, Sally managed a smile that was almost natural. 'Good idea,' she said.

On the way back to the hotel Sally concentrated on pedalling up the hills and on avoiding the traffic and pedestrians; she did not want to think about faithless Althea and Luke's apology. Luke went up to the hotel room with her to get the sweater. Leaving the door ajar, he said deliberately, 'Sally, I have the feeling that no amount of talk is going to solve our problem. Let's go to bed—we'll at least get warm.'

She backed away from him. 'You tricked me—bringing me up here to get a sweater.'

He indicated the half-open door. 'You can leave any time you want.'

So the choice was hers; he would not keep her here against her will. She said foolishly, 'But it's the middle of the day!'

'There's no law against doing it in daylight,' Luke said drily.

A painful blush stained Sally's cheeks. How naïve she had sounded, she thought. How like her mother! And how frightened she was. 'Why do you want to make love to me?' she burst out. 'I'm not what you'd call willing. It's just because you're sorry for what happened last night, isn't it?'

He closed the gap between them, resting his hands lightly on her shoulders. 'Partly, yes. But that isn't the whole reason. I've discovered something the last little while—that I want you very much. I like you. And you're quite astonishingly beautiful, Sally. Although I'm sure you know that without me telling you.'

'But I'm no good in bed!'

Luke hesitated fractionally. 'Who says so?'

'My—someone I knew,' she said lamely.

'Then we have to do our best to prove him wrong, won't we?' He hesitated again; he seemed off-balance to Sally, which surprised her. 'There is something else I'd have to say, though.'

She braced herself. 'Yes?'

'I know one isn't supposed to say this kind of thing, but as far as I'm concerned it's better to be honest.'

Oh, yes, she thought with an hysterical inward giggle, let us by all means be honest. 'What are you getting at, Luke?'

He ran his fingers through his hair, disordering it, so that she was reminded of Caleb. 'If we're lovers while we're here,' he said, 'then we're just that and nothing more. A holiday affair. I don't want commitment. I thought I ought to make that clear to you.'

Conscious of a very confusing mixture of relief and panic, Sally said in a cracked voice, 'Oh—is *that* all? That's no problem at *all*, Luke, I feel exactly the same way. Commitment is the last thing in the world that I want.'

He was visibly disconcerted. 'I thought you'd be upset,' he said slowly.

'Goodness, no!' There could be no mistaking her sincerity, or the brilliance of her smile. 'I wouldn't want it any other way.'

'You're a strange woman,' he said, even more slowly. 'I don't understand you at all.'

'You don't have to,' she answered flippy.

'No, I suppose not.' Restlessly he moved his shoulders. 'So what's your decision, Sally—yes or no?'

Sally stood very still. Luke was between her and the open door, and she had to choose between them. The situation that Lynette had so blithely envisaged had actually arrived: she, Sally, had been given the chance to undo some of the harm of her brief, unhappy marriage and to gamble on a better future. Luke was even prepared to disappear afterwards, just as Lynette had hoped.

She gazed up at him, seeing the strength in his face now that it was divested of bitterness, and the unflinching honesty in his eyes, and suddenly knew what her decision was. Edging around him, she closed the door, snapped the lock and turned to face him, her back to the door. She looked very frightened.

Luke said quietly, 'I don't know what that other man did to you, or who he was, but it went deep, didn't it? You're a brave woman, Sally.'

She could think of nothing to say. Luke patted her shoulder. 'Why don't you take off your shirt and your jeans and lie on the bed, I'll give you a massage. It'll relax you. And if at any time you want me to stop, I promise I will.'

Her movements jerky, as if she were a robot, Sally took off her outer clothes and put them on the chair. Then, wearing a thin T-shirt and her underwear, she lay face down on the bed.

The bed sagged on either side of her as Luke straddled her. He began by stroking the length of her spine with the flats of his hands, spreading them to grasp her shoulders, his movements rhythmical and without hurry, until unconsciously Sally started to relax and her fears began to recede. She offered no resistance when he lifted her T-shirt over her head, instead lying prone enjoying the warmth of his palms on her back, the strength of his fingers as he kneaded the muscles at the base of her neck. Her bra strap was in the way. She unsnapped it herself, felt him ease it over her arms, and closed her eyes again, giving herself over to the almost hypnotic movements of his hands. When they curved around her ribs, brushing the fullness of her breasts, she was ready for him; and when his fingertips found her nipples, she felt again the dart of fire that she had

felt so fleetingly the night before. But this time the tiny
flame grew, fed by Luke's slow, sensuous stroking of
her breasts, until she was engulfed in it. When he lay
down beside her on the bed and said softly, 'Turn over,
Sally,' she obeyed him instantly, her eyes dazed with
wonderment. He cupped her breasts in his hands. He
bent his head and kissed them, and could not have
missed her quiver of response. Still teasing her nipples
in his fingertips, he began kissing her mouth. His eyes
were open, watching her face.

Sally had forgotten fear and relinquished her
inhibitions. But there was an innocence to all her
movements, as though she were doing this for the very
first time, that must have been obvious to Luke; and
when delight, amazement and desire chased across her
face as his kiss deepened, he made a tiny sound in his
throat that could have been compassion. His hands
drifted from her breasts to her hips, removing the last of
her garments then drawing her closer so that she could
not fail to know how much he wanted her.

Sally knew. She wanted him as badly, and with
complete trust opened her thighs to him and smiled
into his eyes. When he touched the moist petals of skin
between her legs, her irises darkened with a fierce and
primitive need. Luke whispered, 'There's no
hurry—we have all the time in the world.'

'But I want you.' With incredulous joy she repeated
herself. 'Luke, I want you! Touch me again—please.'

He did so, watching the storm clouds gather in her
eyes. Then he said, 'Now you touch me, Sally.'

'I'm—not sure how.'

'Anywhere. I guarantee I'll like whatever you do.'

Shyly she began stroking the hair-roughened
contours of his chest, resting her lips where the pulse
throbbed at the base of his throat. He guided her hands
lower to the taut belly, ridged with muscle, and took
the peak of her breast in his mouth. She cried out with

pleasure, instinctively arching her hips against his, and in one smooth, quick thrust felt him enter her.

Briefly panic flared in her eyes. Luke raised his head, holding himself very still, only his hands moving as he touched her with infinite gentleness where she was most sensitive.

She was drowning in a pleasure so overwhelming as to be almost pain. Wrapping her legs around him, she gasped his name and blindly lifted her mouth for his kiss. He began to move inside her. In waves as inexorable as those of the sea the tension mounted, until between one and the next Sally lost all control. Her hips surged to gather him in. The rhythms siezed her, carrying her to a new shore where she had never been before. She felt Luke's release within her, a breaker crashing on the silken sand, and held him close and was one with him . . . and in an immensity of peace felt the tide turn and begin its slow retreat.

For a long time she was silent, for it seemed almost sacrilegious to disturb that peace with the human voice. But eventually she lifted her head from where it was lying on Luke's shoulder and looked into his face. He smiled at her, a smile of such sweetness that her heart turned in her breast.

'It's never been like that for me, Luke,' she stammered. 'Never. I had no idea——' Without warning her eyes filled with tears and her throat closed. She burrowed her face in his chest and wept, crying for the seventeen-year-old girl who had been trapped into marriage with a boy who had not loved her.

Luke held her close until her sobs quietened. Then he said evenly, 'Your turn for explanations, Sally . . . you've had a child, haven't you?' His hand smoothed the faint white lines on her belly.

'Yes.' She sat up, almost glad that he had noticed them, because it forced her into the truth. 'Let me go and wash my face—I'll be right back.'

He brushed a tear from her cheek. 'You don't need to wash your face, you're beautiful as you are.'

Her smile was troubled. 'Was it—was it all right for you, Luke?'

'Oh, Sally.' He folded her in his arms. 'It was wonderful for me! I watched you come alive—an immense compliment to me.'

She gave a sudden throaty chuckle. 'You weren't exactly dead yourself, sir.' She scrambled off the bed and went into the bathroom, where she dashed cold water on her face, blew her nose and for a moment regarded herself in the mirror. Her own face looked back at her, the same, yet subtly altered by a glow of pride and fulfilment.

She walked back into the bedroom, halting as she saw Luke's eyes on her nakedness; he had raised himself on one elbow, the sheets a tangle about his hips. He said, a note in his voice that she had never heard before, 'Your body is exquisite.'

Her shyness vanished in the astonishing knowledge that she would gladly make love to him again. With unconscious grace she knelt on the foot of the bed. 'Yours is beautiful, too,' she said.

'I'd like to spend the rest of the day in bed with you.'

'I was thinking the same,' she said recklessly.

'There are quite a few things we haven't done yet.'

Although she knew she was blushing, she managed just the right tone of insouciance. 'You mean there's more?'

'Much more, my sweet,' he said huskily.

The endearment touched her, for Bruce had not been one for pet names. She said rapidly before she could lose her nerve, 'Luke, I got pregnant in the back seat of a car when I was seventeen. I got married, gave birth to my daughter, and when she was two months old my husband left me. He's the only man I've ever made love to. His name's Bruce.' She ran out of words. Her hands had clenched in her lap, and she made a visible effort to relax them.

'Come over here,' Luke ordered.

She got up and walked around the bed towards him, frightened again. He knew the truth about her now. Maybe he wouldn't want her any more.

He took her hand and pulled her down on the bed to lie beside him, drawing the covers over her to keep her warm and leaving one arm around her. 'Were you able to keep your daughter?'

'Oh, yes! What else would I have done?'

'Lots of people give babies up for adoption.'

'I couldn't have done that!' Her eyes clear as rainwater Sally said simply, 'I love Cecilia more than anyone else in the world.'

Unconsciously Luke's arm tightened around her. 'Did you have any money?'

'Not a cent. We lived with my mother, which enabled me to start up my own secretarial business. I can do that at home, you see.' She added, 'This is the first holiday I've had in five years. My mother died three years ago.'

If Luke was remembering Althea's compulsive, expensive trips, he did not say so. 'So Bruce is the one who left you with the hang-up about sex.'

'Bruce and my mother.' Her brow crinkled. 'My mother was a faithful churchgoer, and yet to me she lived by rules rather than by love. Card-playing, dancing, drinking, sex—they were all out. You got married and bore children because that was your duty as a woman—you weren't meant to enjoy any of it . . . I remember I once gave her a pot of begonias for her birthday, those big, lush red ones with petals that seem to shine in the sun. She didn't water them, and so they died. They were too *alive* for her. Too sensuous, I suppose.' She sighed. 'My whole life was one rebellion after another, because subconsciously I was always afraid I'd end up like the begonias, brown and withered.'

'So the back seat of the car was a rebellion?'

She nodded. 'Bruce was the high-school football hero, and I had a reputation for being wild. He had too much to drink one night after a game, and . . . well, you know what happened. I was willing, don't misunderstand. But afterwards I wished I hadn't been, it was so degrading somehow, a lot of fumbling in the dark that seemed to have nothing to do with me as a person. I vowed never to do it again.' Her smile was wry. 'Two months later when I realised I was pregnant all hell broke loose. Bruce's father and my mother were soulmates—they forced us to get married. Bruce didn't want marriage any more than I did, but he was afraid of his father—and with good reason. But his father got appendicitis when Cecilia was two and a half months old, and that's when Bruce ran away. Went out west.' She finished defiantly, 'I was glad when he went. I hated being married to him as much as he hated being married to me. And he certainly couldn't cope with fatherhood.'

'Would you ever go back to him?'

'Goodness, no!'

'So that's why you were so afraid of an affair.'

'Sex always seemed like a huge conspiracy to me—everyone pretended to enjoy it even though it was really quite dreadful.'

Luke ran his fingers down her ribs. 'Do you still feel that way?'

'You're fishing for compliments.'

'I'll tickle you until you tell me.'

'Two can play that game.' With a boldness she would not have thought possible an hour ago, Sally rippled her nails across his chest, then heard herself say, 'I loved making love with you, Luke—thank you so much.'

He stroked a tendril of hair back from her forehead.

'In view of what you've just told me, last night must have been devastating. I'm truly sorry.'

She smiled at him with all the generosity of her nature.

'You're forgiven. In view of what happened a little while ago.'

With lazy sensuality he caressed the curve of her hip. 'You ain't seen nuthin' yet, lady.'

She gave a breathless laugh and as afternoon faded into evening discovered that she had a great deal more to learn and that learning could be a most pleasurable process. Their lovemaking, begun with laughter, ended in the same tumultuous, uncontrollable storm as before, and afterwards, exhausted, Sally slept.

It was dark when she woke, to find Luke holding her close. 'Didn't you sleep?' she murmured.

'No. I was enjoying watching you.'

'Oh.' She struggled to define his features in the semi-darkness, wondering why she should be disconcerted that he had watched her sleeping after all they had done together in the big bed, wondering too if her concept of marriage was as sterile and restricted as her concept of lovemaking had been. It would be nice to wake in the night with a man's arms around her, and feel this peculiar combination of safety, satiety and excitement. Knowing she did not want to pursue that thought any further, she announced, 'I'm hungry.'

He chuckled. 'There's no satisfying you.'

'Luke! I meant for food. Smoked salmon. Scallops. Crêpes suzettes.'

'How very mundane of you to prefer food to this.' He made a suggestive movement with his hand.

'You're a sex maniac,' she teased.

His voice suddenly sobered. 'Earlier you thanked me, Sally. It's my turn to thank you—being with you has been wonderful for me.'

'I'm glad.' She reached up and kissed his cheek.

His hug drove the breath from her lungs. 'If we have dinner, that'll give us more energy. For later.'

They enjoyed a leisurely meal in one of the other hotels, strolled along the waterfront for half an hour and went back to their room, where in spite of Luke's talk of energy they fell asleep. But in the morning they made love again, with a wild, primitive hunger and in total silence. When it was over Sally smoothed the slick of sweat from Luke's forehead, her fingers not quite steady, for she had not realised she could behave as wantonly as she had.

As if he had read her thoughts, Luke captured her hand in his. 'Look at me, Sally,' he said. Shamefaced, she met the sea-blue eyes. 'Whatever happens betwen us in this bed is right and beautiful,' he said forcefully. 'Do you understand?'

'But I was like a—a wild creature.'

'I loved everything you did. And I'd be willing to bet that's one of the few times in your life you've ever let yourself go and been truly yourself. Am I right?'

'Yes.' Sally bit her lip, suddenly frightened, for in a few days she had to go back home, resume her normal life, and forget the passionate fulfilment she had found in Luke's arms. Stellars Cove and the placid routine of her days seemed a long way away.

Then, through the window they both heard the blare of a band and an outburst of singing. Sally sat up. 'Hey! It's Bastille Day.'

'Changing the subject, Sal?'

She replied with great determination, 'Yes, I am. The sun's shining, Luke—we mustn't waste it.'

Nor did they. A fair had been set up in front of the post office, with rides for the children and stalls selling mussels, ice-cream and balloons. Sailboats dotted the harbour. The cafés were crowded, and impromptu sing-songs echoed from the bars. Clutching a red balloon Luke had bought her, Sally watched him

narrowly lose a contest with a burly St Pierrais to haul
two bales of hay high off the ground with a pulley; he
then shimmied up a pole and brought down the
artificial green parrot from the top, to the applause of
the crowd. They ate lunch with Bev, Dunc, Carol and
Mike, cheered at an egg-and-spoon race in the square,
took a dory to Ile aux Marins, then at dusk munched
meat pies while watching the fireworks burst like
flowers over the dark waters of the harbour. They
finished the day by dancing in the streets until
midnight.

Sally's feet were killing her, for she had swung from
partner to partner and not all of them had been sober;
and someone had spilled wine on the skirt of her sundress. But as she and Luke trailed back to the hotel,
arms around each other in a way she thoroughly
approved, she said, 'I don't know when I've had so
much fun—it was like a big party, wasn't it?'

'And the sun shone all day.'

'Cecilia would have loved the merry-go-round.' Sally
gave a sudden, gaping yawn.

Luke leered down at her. 'None of that—the day's
not over yet.'

'Just as long as I don't have to do anything on my
feet,' she quipped, delighted when he laughed. She
looped her arms around his neck and added
impetuously, 'This has been the best holiday of my
whole life!'

'Sally . . .' There was a funny look on Luke's face.
'You're so different from Althea. *She* took expensive
holidays for granted. As her due. And she had long ago
lost her capacity for enjoyment.'

The street-lamp was shining on his face. 'Do you miss
her, Luke?'

'I did at first. But not now. You've helped heal me,
Sal.'

Knowing she wanted to be naked in his arms in bed

rather than standing on a street corner, Sally said, 'Let's go in.'

His eyes darkened. He bent his head and kissed her, a slow, explicit kiss, murmured against her lips, 'I can't get enough of you,' and a few minutes later in the room proved the truth of his words.

CHAPTER EIGHT

THE next day Sally and Luke went out deep-sea fishing, eating their lunch perched on bait boxes on the deck, the sun glistening on the water. They went back to the hotel and made love before dinner, then went dancing at a couple of the clubs. Sally was consciously avoiding thinking about the end of her stay in three days' time, knowing she was not yet ready to return to Stellars Cove. Or so she phrased it. That she was not telling the strict truth she learned the next morning.

She woke early. Luke was still asleep, lying flat on his back, his left arm flung across her body. In the cool grey light that filtered through the curtains she lay and looked at him. The straight, dark brows, the cleanly sculpted mouth and firm chin were as well known to her as her own features. She watched the steady rise and fall of his chest, remembering the scent of his skin, the strength of his arms, the racing of his heart at the moment of climax. His body had become familiar to her, for she had a hundred images from their lovemaking imprinted in her brain.

You have to go home the day after tomorrow.

And never see him again?

That's right. That was the deal, remember? No commitment. No involvement. A holiday affair and then home again. It was what you wanted, wasn't it?

Yes, it was what I wanted.

But now when Sally pictured her bedroom at home, a room that had always been her sanctuary at the end of the day, she saw it as empty of Luke. No arms around her when she woke in the morning. No passionate lovemaking in the dark. Yet she could not imagine replacing him with anyone else. Dennis? The idea was laughable. Some unknown man whom she would meet in the city? Ridiculous. Luke belonged in her bed. Only Luke.

Suddenly she could not bear her own thoughts. Luke was in her bed now; and she craved closeness. She edged nearer to him and began caressing the curve of his shoulder and the hard line of his collarbone, running her fingers through the tangle of dark hair on his chest. Gradually her hands moved lower.

His eyes still closed, Luke murmured, 'What are you trying to do to me?'

'Seduce you.'

'You're succeeding. Believe me.'

She grew bolder; and she knew by now how to arouse him. As though he sensed her need to assert herself, he lay still under her searching hands, her warm lips, nor did he lose control until she straddled and rode him. As she cried out his name he broke within her, their drowning eyes locked together. Then he drew her down on top of him, holding her close, whispering her name.

Her face was hidden in his shoulder, her eyes squeezed shut. With crystal clarity she heard her inner voice say, You've got to get out of here, Sally. Another two days of Luke's company and you'll be head over heels in love with him.

Don't be silly! I like Luke, certainly, and I love what we do in bed together. But how could I be in danger of falling in love with someone I've only known for a week?

You could. Quite easily.

Sally lay very still, hoping Luke would think she was asleep; and acknowledged the truth in her heart. She could easily fall in love with Luke, because he had the strength and maturity she had always looked for in

Bruce and never found. She and Luke had
circumvented the usual polite approaches between a
man and a woman and had spent a great deal of time in
bed; and there she had learned of his generosity, his
sensitivity and his passion. He had been honest with
her, and caring. He had taught her more than she
would have thought possible; but he had also learned
from her. She could not imagine herself in another
man's arms, and to think of him with another woman
tore her apart.

That little warning voice had been all too accurate.
She *was* in danger.

'You're very quiet,' Luke murmured.

She gave a tiny nod, wishing she could share her
confusion with him, knowing she could not. Because,
for all his care of her, Luke had never once mentioned
the word love, nor had he suggested that the terms of
their affair be any different from those they had started
with. No commitment, no involvement. To burden him
with feelings he did not want would be poor thanks for
all he had done for her.

She said lightly, 'I'm worn out!'

'You could have a sleep this afternoon. Did I tell you
I'm going to the gendarmerie after lunch?'

'They've caught up with you, hmm?'

'Over-indulgence in carnal pursuits.' Luke rubbed his
cheek against her hair. 'Nothing as exciting as that, I'm
afraid. I met the local police chief the other day and
when he found out my job he invited me over. Cognac
and capital punishment.'

The ferry for Newfoundland left St Pierre in the
afternoon. Sally felt her throat tighten. She had been
presented with a perfect opportunity to leave, if that
was indeed what she wanted to do. She wriggled free
of Luke's embrace and with swift grace got out of bed.
'I thought I might go shopping for Cecilia this
morning,' she said casually.

Luke got up as well, inadvertently blocking off her retreat to the bathroom. 'Had enough of me, Sal?' he teased.

With immense effort she kept her face expression less. 'You don't want to trail around the shops looking at teddy bears.'

'I'll buy a paper and wait for you in that little restaurant. The fog's rolled in again by the look of it.'

'OK.' Avoiding his eyes, she edged around him.

He caught her by the arm. 'You're not regretting what you did this morning?'

'No! Of course not.'

'Then give me a kiss before you disappear.'

They were both naked. She wished Luke hadn't used, however innocently, the word disappear. If she caught the ferry this afternoon she would never be held like this again . . . she threw her arms around him and hugged him with all her strength, memorising, for all the many nights she would be alone, the hardness of his body against hers and the warmth of his skin. She felt him take her chin to lift her face and tried to compose her features.

'Sally—it's just a social visit, they're not going to arrest me!'

Infinitely relieved that he had misjudged the cause of her distress, she said, 'Your job worries me sometimes. It seems so dangerous.'

'You've seen too many movies. The only danger this afternoon is that I won't be able to hold my cognac as well as the rest of them.'

'I know. I'm being silly.' She smiled at him weakly.

He gave her a firm kiss that he obviously intended to be reassuring, and a pat on the behind. 'You're sweet to worry. Off you go and shower.'

They repaired to the poky little restaurant for breakfast. The proprietress recognised them by now and called out a greeting, waddling over with their coffee. It was all so normal, thought Sally desperately. So ordinary and yet so frighteningly intimate. She buried her face in the thick china mug, and as soon as she decently could, left Luke alone with his newspaper in the restaurant.

The shops were not as crowded now that Bastille Day was over. Sally soon found a rather charming brown bear dressed in bright yellow oilskins, and a miniature French flag, and knew Cecilia would be happy with both of these offerings. She then purchased her ferry ticket, hiding it in the depths of her handbag as though Luke would be able to see it through the thick brown leather, and trailed back to the restaurant.

Luke was doing the French crossword, frowning prodigiously, his pencil tapping the table. Hidden by the door, Sally watched him for a few moments, a confusion of emotions warring in her breast. She did not want to analyse these emotions; she only knew from their intensity that she was right to leave. She walked over to the table. 'You look as though you need a good brisk walk.'

His grin caught at her heart. 'Nothing like a crossword in another language to keep you humble. Did you find what you wanted?'

She showed him her purchases, excluding the ferry ticket. 'Let's walk over to the airport, I haven't been there.'

'Must be the least used airport in the world.' He gathered up his paper, paid for his coffee, and they headed down the street. 'Don't think I'd like to live in this continual fog. Do you get much in Sydney, Sal?'

Although she had shared with Luke emotions and experiences from her past that she had shared with no one else, not even Lynette, Sally had maintained the fiction of her home in Sydney; somehow Caleb's name had never come up, either. 'Not a lot,' she said, and was glad now she had not told him the truth. When she left this afternoon she had to know she would never see Luke again. It was the only way she would be safe.

They walked at a fast pace around the curve of the harbour to the airport buildings, which were blanketed in low grey cloud. Sally thrust her cold fingers in her pockets. She had had her time in the sun with Luke, she thought sombrely. But now all was obscurity and confusion, a smothering fear like the dull grey clouds. It was time for her to leave. Past time. 'Let's go back,' she said raggedly.

'Sally, is something the matter? You're not yourself today.'

She gave him a false smile. 'I'm fine. Just tired, I guess.'

'Have a rest this afternoon.' Gently he touched the shadows under her eyes with his thumb. 'I haven't been letting you get your sleep. Maybe tonight I should bunk down on the floor!'

Although his words were facetious, his concern was very real. She did not want him blaming himself in any way. She said, 'Luke, you've been wonderful to me—I want you to know that.'

His expression quizzical, he kissed her. 'There are times I don't understand you.'

'How can we understand others when it's so difficult to understand ourselves?' She hunched her shoulders. 'Let's have some of *madame*'s soup before you go to the police station.' Her suggestion had the ulterior motive of keeping her and Luke busy enough that they would not go back to the hotel room together. She did not think she could bear him making love to her again, knowing that it would be for the last time.

Luke draped an arm around her shoulders. 'Soup, and then bed for you,' he said firmly. 'Without me!'

Somehow, keeping up a stream of light conversation, Sally got through lunch. As they left the restaurant, Luke looked down at his jeans. 'I'd better change, since this is a semi-official visit,' he said. So her plan had failed, and once more the two of them went up to the hotel room.

Sally's nerves were stretched tight. As Luke casually pulled his T-shirt over his head and stepped out of his jeans, she found herself staring at his long legs, at the scarred ribs and deep chest, almost as if she had never seen his body before. She turned away and took off her jacket, hanging it over the back of one of the chairs, knowing she would have to hurry once he was gone because the ferry left in less than an hour. It would not take long to pack; and mentally she had already composed the note she would leave.

She sat on the end of the bed to unlace her sneakers, keeping up the fiction that she was going to spend the afternoon resting. Luke was knotting his tie in front of the bathroom mirror, whistling between his teeth. *Yesterday* . . . Sally knew she would never be able to hear that tune again without thinking of him.

He pulled on his tweed jacket and ran a comb through is hair. 'Do I look OK?'

From somewhere she found the strength to say, 'Very handsome. Don't give them every detail of our carnal pursuits, will you?'

'Only if they threaten the rack.' He raised her to her feet, searching her face. 'Have a good rest, won't you, Sal? We'll have a quiet evening tonight.'

Certainly *I* will, she thought miserably. She pulled down his face, kissed him hard on the mouth and said, 'Goodbye, Luke.'

'I'll be back in a couple of hours. I'll try not to disturb you if you're sleeping.' And then he had opened the door and was closing it behind him.

He had gone.

Sally's knees were weak. She sat on the end of the bed again, and absently began to put her sneakers back on. Luke was gone. She would never see him again.

She stood up as abruptly as she had sat down, knowing if she dwelt on those two thoughts she would begin to cry and might not be able to stop. She took her suitcase out of the cupboard, threw it on the bed and began tossing her clothes in. Tears blurring her eyes, she packed her presents for Cecilia, Lynette and Caleb more carefully. Then she took a piece of hotel stationery from the drawer. 'Dear Luke,' she wrote. 'I called home and Cecilia has the flu. Nothing serious, but I feel I should be there. So I'm catching the afternoon ferry. Sorry not to see you to say goodbye, but I know you'll understand. Again, thank you for all you've done for me.'

She paused, chewing on the end of the pen. Then, in a rush, she added, 'I'll never forget you. Sally.'

She folded the notepaper and placed it conspicuously on the bed, closed her suitcase, put on her jacket and without a backward look left the room. At the desk in the lobby she checked out, paying for her share of the room, which largely depleted her stock of francs. Then she hurried down the street towards the ferry dock, casting quick glances over her shoulder, illogically terrified that Luke might appear out of the mist.

He did not. She handed in her ticket, boarded the sleek orange and white boat, and skulked in the cabin utnil the ferry had pulled away from the dock. Through the window she caught a last glimpse of the square where she and Luke had spent Bastille Day. Blindly she stared down at the bag in her lap, fighting back tears.

The rest of the day passed in a blur for Sally; under other circumstances she might have enjoyed the ferry trip, and the van drive from Fortune to St John's through the primitive, spare beauty of the Newfoundland hills. The van dropped her off at the airport, where she was lucky enough to get a stand-by ticket on the last flight to Halifax that evening. She was spending a great deal of money; although she used the bus from the Halifax airport into the city, she took a cab home, knowing she could not face Lynette's questions tonight. Tomorrow she would feel better. She hoped.

It was pitch dark when the cab drew up by her front door. But there were stars piercing the blackness of the sky, promising a clear day tomorrow, and she was suddenly tremendously relieved to be home. This was where she belonged. St Pierre had been a dream-world. This was real.

She had phoned Caleb from the airport, so he was expecting her. He opened the front door, took her case and tried to restrain Sidney from devouring her. 'Down,' he ordered. '*Down*!'

Sidney subsided, his huge jaws agape, his eyes beaming goodwill. Sally looked from him to her brother and said foolishly, '*His* looks haven't improved. but you've grown!'

'Six feet one and a half inches,' said Caleb with great satisfaction, and gave her a clumsy hug. 'How was your holiday, sis? Didn't figure you'd come home early.'

Without warning tears gushed from Sally's eyes. Convulsively she hugged him back and wailed, 'I had a wonderful time! That's the t-trouble.'

Caleb, the rescuer of seagulls and stray dogs, patted his sister comfortingly and said with a new authority in his voice, 'Come on into the kitchen. I'll make you a cup of tea and you can tell me all about it.'

Sally blinked up at him. 'You've changed,' she quavered.

'Well, it's the first time you've ever been away. So even though Lynette was here all day, I still felt I was in charge. I kind of liked it.'

Sally trailed after him into the kitchen, which was extremely neat and clean considering Caleb had not had much warning of her return. 'How's Cecilia?'

'Fine. She missed you at first, but she seems to have got over that. But she'll be really happy to see you tomorrow.'

It is always disconcerting to learn one is not indispensable. Sally sat down at the table, feeling like a stranger in her own kitchen. 'No problems while I was away?' she asked, almost hoping Caleb would answer in the affirmative.

'Nope. Sounds as though you were the one with problems.'

'Well, I met a man, you see, Caleb,' she began hesitantly, not sure how much to tell her brother, for however maturely he might be behaving, he was still only eighteen.

'Did you get in the sack with him?' asked Caleb with genuine interest.

Sally raised her brows, feeling a twinge of sympathy for her mother. '*Really*, Caleb . . .'

'You did, eh? Good for you, sis! Figured you needed a man.'

Sally sat up straight, her tears forgotten. 'Oh, you did, did you?'

'What's he like?' Ignoring her flushed face, Caleb made the tea.

'Once we got an initial misunderstanding sorted out, he was very good to me.'

'Good *for* you, too, I bet.'

'Yes, Dr Dexter,' she said crossly.

'So what's the problem?'

Sally picked up the salt-shaker and examined it with great care. 'I could very well have fallen in love with him, which is why I came home early. So I wouldn't.'

Caleb took a package of cookies from the cupboard. 'What's so awful about falling in love?'

'He didn't want any kind of commitment or emotional involvement. He told me so.' She leaned forward. 'Caleb, I lied to him and said I was from Sydney, so I'm sure he'll never find me here. But if he should ever turn up at the house, you must send him away.'

'Yeah?' Caleb did not look convinced.

'Yes! He doesn't owe me anything, and a clean break is best.' Maybe if she said this often enough she would start to believe it, she thought wretchedly.

'So what's he look like?'

'His name is Luke. He's a bit taller than you, he's got dark brown hair, and his eyes are the same colour as the cove on a sunny day.'

'If he traces you here, it must mean that he's in love with you,' said Caleb with triumphant logic.

'Not necessarily—he's just a nice person who might feel responsible for me in some way. Anyway, he won't arrive on the doorstep, I'm sure he won't. Is there any mail for me?'

I put it in your bedroom. Dennis called a couple of days ago.'

'Oh dear. I know one thing—I'll never marry Dennis.'

'Good,' said Caleb, and passed Sally a cup of tea. 'Sidney chewed your *Time* magazine.'

The subject of Luke did not come up again. Sally went to bed an hour later, fell fast asleep and woke in the night reaching for Luke. Because everything always looks worse in the middle of the night, she cried herself back to sleep, and woke with a start at seven thirty when Cecilia climbed into bed with her, her red curls tickling Sally's chin. Cecilia was extremely happy to have her mother home. Her chubby little arms clamped in a stranglehold around Sally's neck, she burbled away about Sidney chasing the cat next door, and the picnic she had had with Lynette.

Sally held her close, as always struck by wonder at the intensity of her love for Cecilia. She had never loved Cecilia's father, she knew that now, and her pregnancy had been marred by bitterness and strife; yet Cecilia, once born, had relieved Sally of a double burden of guilt and pain by a love so perfect as to be miraculous.

Sally got up half an hour later, producing the French flag and the teddy bear with the yellow oilskins. Caleb had taken advantage of her return to go to work early; at a quarter past eight the telephone rang. Sally picked up the receiver, knowing it could not possibly be Luke, wishing with all her heart that she would hear his deep voice at the other end of the line. 'Sally!' cried Lynette. 'I wasn't expecting to hear your voice. You're home early—how did it go?'

'Fine,' said Sally automatically. 'Cecilia and I are just having breakfast.'

'I'll be over in ten minutes.' And Lynette put down the phone.

Sally signed. Lynette was a sweetheart, but she, Sally, was not ready for an inquisition. Not that she would be any more ready tomorrow, or the day after. Get it over with, she thought stoically, and made herself a cup of very strong black coffee.

Lynette arrived wearing baggy scarlet trousers and an orange shirt, above which her madonna-like beauty seemed even more inappropriate than usual. Sally had made more coffee. She carried the tray outdoors, where she could watch Cecilia in the sand pile constructing towers in which to plant the flag. The sun was shining. The water in the cove was a deep blue-green. Sally tried not to think of Luke and gave Lynette the present she had bought her in St Pierre.

'Stockings from Paris! What fun—thanks.'

'Thank *you* for all your help. Cecilia told me about the picnic.'

'Your delightful daughter is almost enough to make me contemplate matrimony. Almost. Well, come on, Sally—what happened?' Bright-eyed, Lynette peered at Sally over the rim of her cup.

Sally said unhappily, 'I met a man and I had an affair, just as we planned.'

'And you didn't enjoy it,' Lynette groaned. 'Oh,

Sally . . .'

'You're quite wrong. I enjoyed it very much.'

'So why did you come home early? Did he have to leave? Tell me his name and how old he is and what he does for a living—everything about him! I'm dying of curiosity.'

Wishing that today of all days the sky had been cloudy and the cove a leaden grey, Sally said with careful truth, 'He didn't have to leave. I did. Because I'd accomplished what you'd said I should—lost all my inhibitions about sex. As for the rest, his name is Luke, he's thirty years old and he's tall, dark and handsome.' She was not going to tell Lynette Luke's last name any more than she had told Caleb, because she would not put it past either one of them to try to get in touch with him.

To Lynette's continued probing she gave a somewhat edited version of the time she and Luke had spent together and finished by saying flippantly, 'I've proved one thing, that I'll never marry Dennis.'

'Thank goodness for that!' Lynette eyed her shrewdly. 'There's quite a lot you're not telling me.'

'I should hope so,' Sally said decorously.

'Did he fall in love with you?'

'No.'

'You're about as communicative as a clam!' Lynette exclaimed in exasperation. 'When are you going to see him again?'

'I'm not.' Sally refilled Lynette's cup. 'After all, that was the object of the exercise, wasn't it? To have an affair with someone I'd never see again.'

Lynette scowled at her friend. 'I guess so. But I get the impression he was a pretty terrific guy—he must have been, to have undone all the damage caused by Bruce and your mother. Dammit, Sally, forget your pride and give him a chance. Call him up.'

'No, Lynette,' Sally said steadily. 'And the reason I

haven't told you his last name or where he works is so that you won't do it for me.'

Far from being put out, Lynette gave a gurgle of laughter. 'How well you know me! You're sure you're not in love with him?'

'I'm sure,' Sally said. 'Now tell me all the local gossip.'

'Has Caleb told you about the two latest strays?'

Sally looked around as if expecting to see two of Sidney's brothers lolling on the grass. 'What's Caleb done now?'

'He's moving up in the world—from seagulls to children.'

'Lynette! Give.'

'While you've been away he's just about adopted the Bartletts' two children, Neville and Maria. Who are indeed two little strays. Caleb's doing some work for their parents. Mr Bartlett's a composer who could be introduced to you five times a day and still not have any idea who you are. His wife's a singer who wanders around the house belting out arias and looking ethereal, and no wonder because there's never anything in the house to eat. She certainly wouldn't lower herself to be a *hausfrau*. Caleb feels sorry for the two children,' Lynette added ironically, 'surprise, surprise.'

'All Caleb needs is a million dollars and he can pursue a career as a philanthropist.'

'He's not doing badly on sixty bucks a week. Neville's a little hellion, but Maria's rather sweet. She adores Caleb.'

'Thanks for warning me,' Sally said glumly, and went to help Cecilia construct some battlements suitable for the French flag.

About seven o'clock that evening the front doorbell rang. When Sally answered it, Cecilia close on her heels, she knew the identity of the two visitors immediately. The boy, whipcord-thin with burning blue eyes, held out his hand and said politely, 'I'm Neville Bartlett and this is my sister Maria.'

Maria, standing behind him, was wearing a ragged cotton dress, her fine blonde hair in a tangled rope down her back. She was about nine years old and had big grey eyes that went straight to Sally's heart. 'We've come to see Caleb,' she piped.

'I'm Sally, his sister. Please come in,' Sally responded with equal politeness, wondering why Lynette had called Neville a hellion.

Caleb came out of the kitchen, still holding a dishtowel. When he made a pass with it like a bullfighter, Neville exploded into motion. There was a brief, undignified scuffle, which ended with Neville pinned to the floor by Caleb's knee and Caleb saying calmly, 'You didn't hook my ankle quickly enough. Speed is all-important.'

With commendable restraint Sally said, 'Would you mind picking up the magazines that you knocked off the coffee-table?' She didn't see how Caleb could criticise Neville for being slow; she had never seen anyone move so fast.

Caleb said apologetically, 'Neville gets in a lot of fights at school and loses too many of them. So I thought I'd teach him a few tricks. I usually do this outdoors.'

'Good idea,' said Sally. 'Easier on the furniture.'

Caleb grinned. 'There's some casserole left, isn't there, sis? Can I heat it up?'

Sally had already assessed the transparency of Maria's skin and the jut of bones in Neville's wrists. 'Sure,' she said. 'Why do you get in so many fights, Neville?'

'The guys around here think I'm a fairy because my dad's a musician, my mum sings opera, and I'm going to be a dancer. A great dancer.' In another of those whirls of movement Neville pirouetted around the coffee-table, his feet in their worn sneakers bringing music into the room. A split second later he was still again.

But it was not the stillness of repose, Sally decided thoughtfully. It was the stillness of energy contained. Leashed until it was needed. The boy burned with energy. She said equably, 'I'll set the table. I think there was some salad left, too.'

'I hate salad,' said Maria. 'That's all we get to eat at home in the summer. Specially radishes.'

'There might even be two pieces of chocolate cream pie left,' Sally added, a twinkle in her eye, and Maria's thin face lit up.

Cecilia headed for Neville with single-minded determination. Neville might find it necessary to prove his masculinity in the schoolyard, but he was perfectly content to have Cecilia sitting adoringly on his knee. Realising there was more to the Bartlett children than met the eye, Sally began cutting some big slabs of French bread.

CHAPTER NINE

THE summer days passed, bathed in sunshine or cooled by rain, soothed by the ceaseless lap of waves in the cove, brightened by the flowers in Sally's garden. Sally was very busy. Because her precipitate departure from St Pierre had cost her extra money, she had advertised for work in the newspaper and posted her name at all the universities where summer sessions were in progress, and after a hiatus of four or five days was swamped with reports, letters and essays. Caleb was working most of the day, so she also had the care of Cecilia, although in this she was often helped by Neville and Sidney; Maria, however, was content to curl up in a corner with a succession of Sally's childhood books. The individual days almost always seemed long to Sally, and the nights longer, for she was tormented by dreams of Luke, some of them so graphically erotic that she was ashamed of herself, all of them haunted by a sense of loss. Nevertheless, the summer seemed to be flying by, July slipping past as she typed several chapters of a doctoral thesis, August entering with a pile of form letters for a local charity and some handwritten lecture notes from a history professor, who might be an expert on seventeenth-century warfare but whose vowels and consonants were entangled on the page like peasants on a battlefield.

Sally was glad to be busy. More and more her affair with Luke began to seem like a dream, even a dream that had happened to someone else. Her body might ache for him at night; subconsciously she might search for him among the crowds on the city pavements; but he never appeared, either in her bed or on the street, and she was beginning to realise that he never would. Her strategy had worked. Her lies had deceived him. Luke had vanished from her life.

She was not really aware of how bereft she often looked, her grey eyes clouded by unhappiness even while they were perplexed that she should feel so unhappy. She did not love Luke. So why should she miss him?

She sometimes felt as though she had exchanged one prison for another. In the three years after Bruce had left she had been unable to reach out to another man for fear. Now she was unable to reach out because she was ensnared by memories of Luke: the laughter in his sea-blue eyes, the note in his voice when he wanted to make love to her, his naked body reaching for her across the bed. No other man interested her. Not the history professor, even though he was young and had a nice smile; not Dennis, whom she was no longer dating; not any ideal man whom she could conjure up in her fantasies. Her first rebellion at the age of sixteen had given her Cecilia. Her second had left her bound to a man she would never see again. Rebellion number three, she vowed, would be a long time coming.

Caleb was not so absorbed in his jobs for the various families of Cranberry Head and his championing of Neville and Maria that he did not see his sister's unhappiness. One fine Sunday towards the end of August he said to Sally, 'There's a band concert at the Public Gardens this afternoon. Let's take Cecilia and go. I'll treat you both to an ice-cream afterwards.'

'But I should finish printing that——'

'It'll keep. C'mon, sis, you look like the last rose of summer.'

'Thanks a lot!'

'I tell it like I see it . . . you still moping for that guy from St Pierre?'

'No! Of course not. I was right to leave there,' Sally replied, hoping her words did not sound as hollow as they felt. 'Shall we take Neville and Maria?'

'Nope. Just the three of us. Put on your sundress, why don't you?'

She had not worn the sundress since Bastille Day. 'All right, I will,' she said emphatically. 'Cecilia can feed the ducks.'

The gardens were in the centre of the city, surrounded by a wrought-iron fence and ablaze with dahlias, roses and begonias. Sally found a bench in the shade of an ornamental tree, not so close to the bandstand that she was caught up in the crowds, but close enough to enjoy the popular tunes the band was playing. In the intermission the three of them strolled closer to the pond, where pigeons and ducks jostled for crumbs. Cecilia ran ahead. Sally lagged behind to admire an immensely tall stand of dahlias, taller than herself, the flowers like shaggy heads with big yellow eyes. She looked around for Caleb to show him the glorious gradations of pink and gold in some of the petals, and saw a man standing beneath a linden tree staring at Cecilia. A man with thick hair and sea-blue eyes. Luke.

Instinctively she drew back among the dahlias, hiding her red hair among the brazen blossoms. She was scarcely thirty feet away from him, close enough to see the stunned look on his face as he gazed at her daughter's flaming red curls and big grey eyes. He took two steps towards Cecilia, hunkered down beside her and croaked, 'Is your name Cecilia?'

Cecilia was firing scraps of bread at a green-winged duck. 'Cecilia Ruth Cowan,' she said. 'Here duckie, duckie.'

Sally watched the muscles move in Luke's throat. he was wearing an open-necked shirt with canvas trousers, and looked devastatingly handsome; she tucked herself a little more securely among the dark green leaves and heard his ask, 'Is your mummy here?'

Cecilia looked around vaguely, plainly not interested. 'Somewhere . . . d'you like ducks?'

'I like the white ones with the orange beaks. Do you live in Halifax, Cecilia?'

'Stellars Cove, Hal'fax, Nova Scotia,' Cecilia chanted; she had been taught this by Sally, who had also endeavoured to teach her not to talk to strangers. Cecilia held out a chunk of dry bread. 'You can feed them, too,' she said.

'Thank you,' Luke said gravely.

From the corner of her eye Sally saw Caleb approach the pair feeding the ducks. The brown duck waddled away from him, Cecilia in hot pursuit. As Luke straightened Caleb said politely, 'Any problem here?'

'Are you with Cecilia?'

Caleb nodded, his expression neutral.

'My name is Luke Sheridan. I met Cecilia's mother in St Pierre.'

With perfect composure Caleb held out his hand. 'How do you do? Sally told me about you—I'm Bruce Cowan.'

Luke droped the proffered hand as if it had stung him and said hoarsely, '*Who*?'

'Bruce Cowan—Sally's husband. Cecilia's father.'

'You and Sally are divorced. She told me so!'

'I came east for a visit while she was away. We've decided to get together again.' Caleb gave Luke an engaging smile which Luke did not return. 'We figure we can make it now. Older and wiser and all that. Besides, it'd be a lot better for Cecilia.' He glanced over his shoulder. Cecilia was standing by the railings at the edge of the pond, waving at the swans.

Luke's mouth was a grim line. 'Sally told me she'd never go back to you.'

'No accounting for women, is there?' Caleb drawled.

'Look, it's been nice talking to you. But I'd better grab that kid before she falls in the pond.' He raised a hand in careless salute. 'See you.'

Luke stood still in the middle of the path, his face drained of expression. People eddied around him, some of them eyeing him curiously. For a full minute he stayed where he was, watching Cecilia and the blond-haired man at her side; the child had tucked her hand confidently in the man's and was chattering away to him. Then the man swung the child into his arms as one of the swans came a little too close. Slowly Luke turned and walked away from them, passing on the other side of the tall stand of dahlias, his hands thrust in his pockets and his feet scrunching the loose gravel in the path.

Sally let out her breath in a long sigh. She had told Caleb to send Luke away if he ever showed up; and Caleb, with fiendish ingenuity, had done just that. Luke now had her address. But she knew him well enough to know that he would never seek her out if he thought she was back with Bruce. She edged around the dahlias and saw his tall figure disappear behind a hedge of hydrangeas.

Cecilia was now perched on Caleb's shoulders, the two of them following the stately progress of a swan along the path. But Sally was not yet prepared to face either one of them. She cut across the grass and headed for the concrete bridge over the goldfish pond. Leaning her elbows on the bridge, she gazed down into the murky green water. Her heart was racing and her hands were cold, almost as if she had just witnessed a traffic accident.

A brilliant orange fish was finning lazily among the reeds. She should have faced Luke herself rather than letting Caleb do it for her? Or had she been wise to remain hidden? What good would it have done to have talked to Luke again? Re-opening old wounds, exposing all her pain and indecision . . .

A pair of tanned forearms rested themselves on the concrete parapet beside her. She would have recognised those hands anywhere; they were gripping the bridge as if they would like to pick it up and fling it into the water. Slowly she raised her eyes. 'Hello, Luke,' she said.

'I figured you had to be somewhere around. Did you witness that charming little scene between me and Bruce?' He did not wait for an answer. 'Of course you did. you were skulking among those dahlias, weren't you? Hiding from me.' His smile was thoroughly unpleasant. 'Not that I blame you. I'd be hiding too, if I were you.' He mimicked her voice with savage emphasis. *'Oh, I could never go back to my husband.* Didn't take you long to change your mind, did it, Sal?'

She restrained herself from wrapping her fingers around his wrist and said, 'Why do you care, Luke?'

'Because you lied to me!' he snarled. 'From beginning to end you lied to me. You've never lived in Sydney in your life, have you?'

'No.'

'Stellars Cove, Halifax County, Nova Scotia . . . you'd be very amused by what a fool I made of myself last month. Took off to Sydney, searching for you the length of Prince Street, called up every Cowan in the telephone book, and finally came to the conclusion—not for the first time in my life, as well you know—that I was a gullible idiot.'

'No, I wouldn't be amused,' she said quietly; this was far worse than she could have expected.

'Then why did you lie, Sally? Why did you leave that explanatory little note on the bed—nice touch, that—saying Cecilia had the flu? Cecilia didn't have the flu! You'd phoned home and found out Bruce was back, hadn't you?'

His voice had risen. She said flatly, 'We're attracting

attention.'

Luke scowled venomously at the inoffensive couple who had stopped to watch the goldfish and seized Sally by the arm, a move that regrettably sent a shaft of fire through her body. He hustled her off the bridge to a little *cul de sac* of rose bushes beside the wrought-iron fence, dropped her arm much as he had dropped Caleb's hand, and continued as if there had been no interruption. 'You couldn't wait to get in bed with him, could you? Show him everything I'd taught you!'

Her face paled. If Luke had taken a knife and driven it into her he could not have hurt her more deeply. She said in a thin voice, 'I don't know why you're so angry. You didn't want commitment, you said so yourself.'

'I didn't expect you to go from my bed to your former husband's within twenty-four hours!'

She rubbed at her forehead. This was ridiculous. It had to stop. 'Luke,' she said, 'I know I lied to you about——'

'I though you were different,' he interrupted bitterly. 'I genuinely thought you were different. You'd look at me with those big grey eyes of yours and I'd believe every word you said. I loathe generalisations, but by god, I'm beginning to believe there's no such thing as an honest woman. A woman you can trust. First Althea, and now you——'

'I'm *not* like her!'

'You lied about where you live. You lied about your husband. You lied about your reasons for coming home. Three lies in a week. Not bad, Sally. Althea would have had a hard time keeping up with you.'

Incensed, she cried, 'I'm beginning to think *you* lied when you said no emotional involvement!'

'As you're back with your husband we'll skip any discussion about my involvement or lack of it,' Luke snapped. 'There's just one other thing.'

Sally had time to think how incongruous he looked

with his furious face framed by drooping pink roses before he grabbed her, bent his head and kissed her.

It was a kiss more noted for brevity than subtlety, a truly impressive mixture of rage and raw hunger; a hunger which Sally more than matched with all the pent-up needs of the last month, all the times she had woken in the night reaching for his body. Then Luke had wrenched himself free of her. He grated, 'You'd better reconsider this wonderful reconciliation with Bruce. Or are you promiscuous as well as a liar?'

Scarcely able to stand, Sally watched him brush past the rose bushes and stride down the path that led to the big iron gates. The heavy-petalled roses bobbed on their stems and then were still.

She wanted to bury her face in their fragrant faces and weep. She wanted to rip the petals from the bushes and stamp them into the ground. She wanted to make love with Luke and have him sprinkle rose petals on her skin . . . oh, God, how she wanted him!

Being a law-abiding young woman, she left the roses where they were and hurried along the path towards the pond, which fortunately was in the opposite direction from that which Luke had taken. Cecilia was now chasing the plump-breasted pigeons; she must have run out of bread. Caleb was leaning against a nearby tree, chewing gum. he waved when he saw Sally, his teeth gleaming in a wide smile. 'Did you hear what I said to your friend Luke?'

'I did.'

'I handled that pretty well, didn't I?' he crowed. 'Never knew I had it in me.'

Neither did she. She said evenly, 'What made you say you were Bruce?'

'Pure inspiration! I knew right away he was the guy you didn't want to see again, so I figured if I pretended to be Bruce that'd get rid of him.'

'You succeeded beyond your wildest expectations.'

Caleb's smile faded. 'You said you wanted me to get rid of him.'

Sally's shoulders had a forlorn droop in her pretty sundress. 'I know. But he was furious.'

'You mean he saw you?'

'Oh yes. We've just had a very vocal and very public disagreement.' Although brawl would be a more accurate word.

'Oh,' Caleb said helplessly. 'I'm sorry, sis.'

'You did what I asked you to do—you shouldn't have to apologise.'

'Want to go home?'

Tears pricked her eyelids. 'No,' she said. 'We'll listen to the rest of the concert and then we'll buy ice-creams. Just as we planned.' Maybe she would see Luke again. And this time, instead of gaping at him like a stranded goldfish, she would explain.

Explain that you were afraid of falling in love with him, Sally?

Well, maybe I wouldn't have to go quite that far . . .

But Sally was not given the chance to explain anything, because she did not see Luke again. Not in the gardens nor on the busy street corner where they queued up for ice-cream. She had no idea why he was in Halifax or where he was staying, and while he had her address she would wager her new word-processor that he would not seek her out. All this she poured out to Lynette when the latter dropped by for tea that evening. 'I'll never have an affair again!' Sally wailed. 'He thinks I'm a liar and a cheat.'

'He should know you better than that.'

'I did lie to him.'

'Self-protection. Excusable under the circumstances.'

Sally remembered the harsh lines in Luke's face. 'Not by him.'

'Pooh! If he's half the man you say he is, he'll give you a fair hearing. Wait until the morning and phone him at his place of work—which I'm sure you know even if you haven't told me or Caleb.'

'I couldn't possibly do that,' Sally murmured, and on Monday morning found the number of the parole board from directory enquiries and dialled it with fingers that shook. 'May I speak to Luke Sheridan?' she asked the receptionist who answered the phone.

'Mr Sheridan's on leave of absence until Christmas, ma'am.'

Sally gulped. 'Do you have a forwarding address?'

'Not yet, no. He'll be based in Halifax as far as I know.'

Sally said hollowly, 'Thank you,' and rang off. To know that Luke would be living in Halifax was infinitely worse than having him safely in New Brunswick. What if she met him with another woman?

This thought was so upsetting that she punched the wrong key, lost the file she had been working on, and had to start all over again. She made more mistakes the rest of the day than she would normally make in a week. At a quarter past four when the doorbell rang she was still in her office, putting the finishing touches to the history professor's latest lecture. Sidney began to bark, for he took his duties as watchdog all too seriously. Sally yelled at him to be quiet, Cecilia imitated her in her most piercing voice, Neville turned up the music for *Les Sylphides* another notch and Caleb shouted, 'I'll go, sis!'

Sally glanced at her watch, wondering who it could be. Whoever it was would be frightened off before he got thorugh the door. Sidney was still barking. She ran her fingers through her hair in exasperation, pushed back her chair and went into the living-room. 'Sidney, be *quiet*!' she cried, just as Caleb opened the front door.

Luke was standing on the step. Ignoring Sally, he said to Caleb, '*Sis*? Would you be referring to Sally by any chance? Or did you bring your sister with you to help rebuild your marriage?'

Sidney stopped barking. There was a small, dreadful silence, during which Caleb flushed scarlet. Sally said loudly, 'He's my brother. Not my husband.'

'I see,' Luke said smoothly. 'Then perhaps we'd better be reintroduced. Unless there are two Bruces in the family—that *would* be a coincidence.'

Caleb was still struck dumb. Sally said defiantly, 'His name is Caleb. Caleb Dexter. When I came home from St Pierre I told him if by any chance you ever traced me here that he was to send you away . . . I just hadn't quite anticipated his method.'

'Well, it worked,' Luke rejoined, giving Caleb a considering look. 'Very effective.'

Caleb finally found his voice. 'I owe you an apology.'

'Yes, I believe you do. And then your sister owes me an explanation.'

'I don't owe you anything!' Sally exclaimed.

Luke directed the whole force of his personality at her. 'I'm not leaving here until you tell me why you left St Pierre. So unless you want me camped on your front lawn, you'll have to start talking.' Then, taking his time, he surveyed everyone in the room.

Sidney had subsided on his haunches, his hairy tail swishing back and forth on the tile floor; once strangers were in the door, Sidney treated them as members of the family. Sally was frozen in place by the office door. Cecilia, surrounded by mutilated magazines, for she had been pasting pictures in her scrapbook, gave Luke her most capitvating smile. Neville, with his usual air of barely contained energy, was regarding him unsmilingly from beside the record player, while Maria paid him no attention whatsoever.

'I thought you said one child,' Luke remarked to Sally.

'In that, I told the truth.'

'So introduce me to everyone.'

'My brother Caleb you've already met——'

'Twice now,' Luke said imperturbably, glancing over at Caleb, who said in a rush, 'I shouldn't have pretended to be Bruce. But Sally had told me she didn't want to see you again, and I thought pretending to be Bruce was a brilliant way of getting rid of you.'

'Brilliant,' Luke concurred. 'You had me convinced for the best—or I should say the worst—part of the day. Cecilia I've also already met.'

Sally said evenly, 'The dog is Sidney, the young man by the record player is Neville Bartlett, son of a neighbour, and his siter Maria is reading in the corner.' She stopped, her mind a total blank.

Luke looked around. The room was comfortable, shabby, untidy, but very clean. A bowl of garden flowers stood on a table by the big picture window that overlooked the cove; two cats were slumbering in the far corner of the chesterfield. Sally could not have known he was making an inward comparison with the luxurious and artistically arranged furnishings that Althea had always insisted were her due, and among which she would not have allowed either children or pets. This room would never be featured in a glossy magazine; but it said a lot about Sally. He remarked, 'There doesn't seem to be much privacy for you and me to have a heart-to-heart talk, Sally. Even less for a damned good fight—which is what I feel like right now.'

'There is never any privacy. And I don't want a fight.'

'I'm going to find out why you left St Pierre.'

The man who stood in front of her was the man who had survived a hostage-taking. Sally raised her chin. 'To avoid scenes like this.'

'It's too late for avoidance, Sal.' He advanced a couple of paces. 'If you don't want to fight, you could at least give me a kiss—for old times' sake.'

Briefly she closed her eyes, her face a mask of pain.

'Don't, Luke,' she whispered. 'Please don't.'

'So St Pierre did mean something to you.'

'Of course it did!'

'You'll forgive me if I was beginning to wonder. Get rid of everyone for five minutes, Sally. You owe me that much, surely.'

Panic seized her by the throat. 'Don't go, Caleb!' she gasped.

Caleb took a step forward and with his new air of maturity said to Luke, 'Sally has a right to be left alone if that's what she wants.'

There was another charged silence, during which Sidney wagged his tail and Caleb held Luke's gaze. Then Luke said with a complete lack of emotion, 'I suppose she does. Sally, is that what you really want—for me to leave you alone? Is that why you left St Pierre? Because if it is, then I'll go. And I won't come back.'

His voice might be devoid of emotion. But Sally was not deceived. Anger and frustration were churning in his blue eyes; less easily recognisable was fear. She drew a deep breath, aware that everyone in the room, including Sidney, was staring at her. 'Caleb got some fresh haddock from one of the fishermen today,' she said. 'Why don't you stay and have supper with us?'

Luke's shoulders sagged, and something tight-held in his face relaxed. 'I'd like that,' he said.

The tension in the room evaporated. Caleb said cheerfully, 'I'll peel the potatoes, sis,' Neville put on another record, and Cecilia waved a book of fairy-tales at Luke. 'Read me a story?'

'Sure,' said Luke. 'Unles your mother wants help in the kitchen.'

Sally was quite sure she would fry the vegetables and boil the haddock if Luke were to be in the kitchen with her. 'Keeping Cecilia amused would be a big help,' she said diplomatically and fled into the kitchen. Ten minutes later when she peered into the living-room Luke was seated on the chesterfield, Cecilia curled up on one side, the cats on the other, and Maria perched on the arm. His deep voice was extracting the maximum pathos from Cinderella's plight by the fireside, while Neville, congenitally unable to sit still, was acting out the three ugly sisters and the beautiful Cinderella, his face and body movements bringing them all to startling life. Sally went back to grating cabbage for coleslaw, aware of a swift, dizzying upsurge of happiness that Luke should be here. Although she had no idea why he was in Halifax or why he had sought her out today, and although she knew a confrontation between them was inevitable, nothing could dim this happiness.

Rather to Sallys surprise the meal she had prepared was excellent, from the crispy fried haddock and the home-grown vegetables to the blueberry pie, made from berries Maria had picked out on the headland. There was an ease between Caleb and Luke that she envied, because she found her own gaze had a tendency to skitter away from Luke's; the two men carried the conversation at the dinner-table. The subject moved to Luke's job as a parole officer in New Brunswick. Neville had been shovelling his food in as if this might be his last meal; he swallowed a piece of potato and said scornfully, 'The guys in prison are the stupid ones. They got caught.'

'Some of them have low IQs, certainly,' Luke agreed. 'And a large percentage are illiterate. But not all of them are stupid. Are you saying crime is OK as long as you don't get caught?'

'If I committed a crime,' Neville boasted, 'I'd plan it carefully enough that I wouldn't get caught.'

Luke took a drink of water. 'What sort of crime would you commit?'

'I'd rob a bank.'

'What would you do with the money.'

Neville's lashes flickered. 'Take ballet lessons.'

Sally held her breath. This was no longer polite dinner conversation, for Neville, restless, talented Neville, was openly challenging Luke. Luke said calmly, 'I would suspect very few if any of the major dancers of this century have found it necessary to rob a bank.'

'My mum and dad don't have any money.'

'There are scholarships.'

'If you've got lots of money you get better teachers.'

'You have to earn the right to better teachers.'

'I'm going to be the best,' said Neville unwinkingly.

'So what have you done so far towards that goal?' Luke persisted.

'I took lessons in Halifax last year. But I couldn't go to the summer camp because we didn't have the money and dad said scholarships were demeaning. So I've got to have my own money.'

Sally kept quiet. She had not known about the dance camp. Luke said flatly, 'Don't steal the money, Neville—that's a dead-end street. They don't teach ballet in the pen.'

Neville's eyes dropped first. He looked down at his plate and said, 'Can I have some more fish, Sally?'

Sally passed the fish, Caleb asked a question about Luke's university background, and the talk subsided to normality. After dinner they played a game of Monopoly, which Neville won. Then Sally got Cecilia ready for bed, Luke listened to the ritual bedtime story. Sally kissed her daughter goodnight, switched out the light and left the room. The hall was dimly shadowed. Luke said softly, 'Come here, Sally.'

It did not occur to her to disobey. She lifted her face wordlessly as his arms slid around her waist. His lips met hers in what she might have called tenderness had it not so swiftly turned to passion. She clutched at him, exulting in the probe of his tongue, his fierce caresses, so well remembered, so steeped in knowledge.

From downstairs Maria called Sally's name, and it was as if the voice were from another planet. With a reluctance so strong that it was almost a physical pain Sally pulled free of Luke. 'I've got to go,' she stammered.

She was wearing an open-necked blouse; the pulse was racing in the hollow of her throat. Luke said, his voice almost normal, '*That* hasn't changed.'

Again Maria's call floated up the stairs. Sally pushed herself away from Luke's chest, as if she were launching herself into unknown waters, and stumbled down the stairs.

Maria and Neville were ready to go home. Caleb looked at Sally's flushed cheeks and said, 'Why don't you and Luke walk them home? I'll stay with Cecilia.'

'Sure,' said Luke, from behind Sally,. 'we'll walk them home.'

So the stage was set for the confrontation.

CHAPTER TEN

THE sun had sunk almost to the horizon in a flare of red and orange; daubed with the same colours, the waters in the cove swayed gently with the tide. As Luke and Neville lagged behind, so that their low-voiced conversation was inaudible to Sally, Maria tucked her hand in Sally's and began relating the plot of *The Yearling* to her in confused detail. Maria did not show much affection, perhaps because she got so little at home; Sally listened carefully, putting in a question every now and then.

The road climbed to the headland with its ancient glacial rocks among hunched trees and low-growing shrubs. The wind blew off the Atlantic, carrying gulls with spread wings whose cries keened over the waves. The Bartlett house was at the very end of the road. The garden needed weeding; and although Caleb had worked manfully at repairs, the house gave the impression that a strong wind might blow it down. A single light shone from a room under the eaves.

Sally had met the Bartletts. Neville's mother, having failed to establish a career as an opera singer, had instead made a life's work of being temperamental; Mr Bartlett, perhaps in reaction, was vague in the extreme. She did not expect either of them to greet Maria and Neville now, nor did they. The children disappeared inside, and Luke and Sally turned back. Luke shoved his hands in his pockets. 'Unless someone exercises some control over that kid, he's going to end up in trouble,' he said. 'Don't misunderstand me—you and and Caleb have been good for him. But he's got so much damn energy!'

Sally managed to keep the conversation on Neville and Maria all the way to the fork in the road that was a few hundred yards from her house. But there Luke seized her by the hand and pulled her towards the left-hand track. 'That goes to the wharf,' she protested.

'I know. I want to find a place where we can talk.'

'Caleb's expecting me home——'

'A fairly public place, so I'll keep my hands off you.'

She found herself accompanying him down the left-hand track as if she were a rag doll without will of her own. The wharf was deserted, although a Cape Islander was moored alongside. Sally sat down on the hard concrete, dangling her feet over the edge, remembering all the times she and Caleb had fished for mackerel with scraps of bacon on jigging hooks. The lights of Stellars Cove shimmered on the water. It was very quiet.

Luke sat down beside her, his body not touching hers. 'Before I start,' he said calmly, 'let me make one thing clear. I'm in Halifax for at least the next four months—I'm on special leave from the parole board to teach a couple of courses on criminology at St Mary's—and I want to keep on seeing you. No question of that.'

Sally thought of several replies ranging from the flip to the obscene, and said none of them. 'Don't the lights look pretty on the water?' she remarked.

Luke ignored this. 'I'm sure you know what I'm going to ask you,' he said. 'Why did you leave St Pierre, Sally?'

She was banging her heels against the wooden abutments of the wharf. After a silence that had stretched on too long, she said, 'I was running away. Running away from exactly the sort of thing that's going on now.'

'I'm not the Grand Inquisitor, Sal. I'm the man whose bed you shared—remember?'

She ducked her head. 'Yes, I remember.'

'Look at me.' Unwillingly her head swung around.

'Making love with you was the best thing that's happened to me in a long time,' he said deliberately. 'Wasn't it good for you? Is that why you ran away?'

His face gave nothing away. But because she knew him well, she knew a part of him was afraid of her reply. She said with total honesty, 'Apart from Cecilia, it was the best thing that ever happened to me.'

Het let out his breath in a long sigh. 'You had me worried.'

His admission touched her to the heart. 'I'm no actress, Luke. I couldn't possibly have faked my responses to you.'

'Then why did you leave?'

She held his gaze, her eyes as dark as the night sky behind her, and knew he deserved an honest answer. 'Because I liked making love with you too much—I was beginning to need it. I can't afford that. So I ran away.'

'My God,' Luke said.

The sea sloshed among the pilings at the end of the wharf; the hum of traffic came from the highway across the cove. Sally kept silent, for the only thing she could add was *I was afraid I might fall in love with you*, and those were words she did not want to say.

'I thought up a lot of reasons,' Luke said finally, 'but that was never one of them.' With a careful lack of emphasis he went on, 'Under those circumstances why don't we just continue?'

'Continue what?' she said blankly.

'Making love, Sally,' he said, as if he were stating the obvious.

Unconsciously she increased the space between them. 'No! No, I couldn't do that.'

'Why not! We're two adults and we both enjoy it.'

'Luke, I was on *holiday*.'

'The world's population would not be increasing at the rate it is if people only made love on holidays.'

'Don't be funny! You know what I mean—this is real life. This is where I live. I've got a four-year-old daughter and an eighteen-year-old brother and a very small house with no privacy and nosy neighbours—I can't have an affair here!'

'I'll have an apartment in town with all kinds of privacy.'

'Luke, I *can't!*'

Before she guessed his intention he reached across, nuzzled his face into her neck and left a trail of kisses that burned like fire. He must have felt her shiver of response. He said roughly, 'I could change your mind.'

She bent her head. 'You'd be using the most unfair of weapons,' she said in a low voice.

'Would I? Or am I merely confronting us with the truth? That we want each other.'

'I can't have another affair with you,' she repeated stubbornly. 'Maybe you understand now why I lied to you about Sydney—so I'd avoid this kind of scene.'

He said slowly, 'You're still running, Sally.'

'If I am, that's my choice.'

Her profile was turned to him with its straight nose and set jaw. 'We're only talking about four months,' he said. 'I'm not asking you for a lifelong commitment.'

That's the problem. Sally shoved the words back into her subconscious where they belonged. 'I can't,' she said.

There was a long pause. A motorbike revved up across the cove, then sputtered into silence. The Cape Islander bumped against the rubber tyres strung to the wharf. Sally listened to the beat of blood in her ears and remembered with agonising clarity the smoothness of Luke's shoulder under her palm, his searching, sensitive fingers at her breast. *I can't . . . I can't.*

'OK,' said Luke. 'Then how about this? I'm at a loose end the next couple of weeks. I'm staying with my friend John Sayles for a week, then I'm moving into my apartment. Classes don't start until the seventh of September. I think Cecilia's a darling, Caleb's a fine young fellow, and I'd like to keep an eye on Neville . . . will you let me hang around? Drop in sometimes and visit you?'

'I have to work.'

'You work very hard, Sally,' he said gently.

'It pays the bills.'

'With very little left over for you, I'd be willing to bet.'

'Don't feel sorry for me, Luke!'

'I don't. I admire you—you're a good person.'

She knew he meant every word he said. She reached out and rested her hand on his arm as lightly as the sea breeze might have brushed his skin; it was the first time she had touched him voluntarily that day. 'Thank you,' she said, and was further disarmed when he gave her the smile he had always saved for their most intimate moments.

As he cleared his throat, Sally snatched back her hand. 'Well . . . to get back to my proposal,' he said. 'I could help out, Sally. Take Cecilia off your hands when you're working. Mow the lawn. Make myself useful. And I promise I won't try to drag you off to the nearest bed,' he finished lightly.

His tone of voice troubled her. 'I'm not playing games!' she said. 'I can't have an affair with you here, Luke, it wouldn't work. If you can't accept that, you'd better stay away.'

He answered her with equal seriousness. 'I don't like your terms, Sally—but I accept them. I swear I'll do nothing towards resuming our affair.'

'You mustn't even kiss me,' she insisted, knowing she sounded ridiculous but unable to help herself.

'I'll visit you as a friend and help out where I can. That's all.'

How could she refuse such a reasonable request without being churlish? For Neville's sake alone, she should agree. She frowned at him and said ungraciously, 'I suppose that would be all right.'

'Great,' Luke said as casually as if they had been discussing the price of fish. 'Now I'm going to get up before this concrete cripples me for life.'

Sally scrambled to her feet, not wanting him to touch her. They walked to the house, where Luke poked his head through the door to call goodbye to Caleb. Then he got into his car. 'Night, Sally. I'll probably see you tomorrow.' A quick salute of his hand and he drove away.

Sally watched him go, feeling frightened and frustrated in equal measure. She should never have agreed to his plan, however reasonable it had sounded. She could not have analysed all the complicated feelings Luke aroused in her, but she knew one thing: none of them were reasonable.

Luke dropped in, as he phrased it, every day of the following week. He met Lynette and the two of them got along famously. Cecilia began to count on his presence, abandoning her mother with heartless joy whenever Luke arrived and spending hours with him in the garden. Sally should have been pleased that Cecilia was not under foot, and pleased also that Luke was keeping so scrupulously to his bargain: he never as much as took Sally's hand or kissed her on the cheek, let alone tried to drag her off to bed. But she was not pleased. She was irritable and short-tempered, which drove her to behave towards Luke with artificial politeness; every time she did so in Caleb's presence, her brother looked at her with a puzzled frown that irritated her further. She took to going for long walks by herself in the evenings then staying up to watch the late movies on television, eating too many chips and drinking too much coffee. None of these measures soothed her nerves.

The last day of August was still and very hot, a huge pale sun in a pale blue sky, the sea with the dead calm that sometimes presages a storm. Sally had received another batch of the history professor's scribblings; her familiarity with his handwriting did not seem to increase its legibility, so consequently she should have been concentrating on her work. But how could she concentrate when her blouse was sticking to her back and when Luke was out in the garden in nothing but a pair of running-shorts? He was playing with Cecilia; the sight of her daughter's red curls resting so confidently on Luke's bare chest produced a peculiar pain in the vicinity of Sally's heart. She knotted her blouse viciously tight beneath her breasts and went back to the study. An hour later, thoroughly incensed by the professor's inability to differentiate the letters n, r and m, she stormed into the kitchen to get some lemonade. She did not see Luke, who had been in the kitchen, until she collided with a hair-roughened torso and spilled lemonade on it. The scent of his skin filled her with an agony of desire. She exclaimed, 'Oh, *damn*!' and burst into tears.

Luke took the glass from her hands, put it on the counter and said, 'I can't hug you, I'll cover you with lemonade . . . don't cry, Sally love.'

'I'm *not* your love!' she sobbed. 'I should never have got out of bed this morning—why can't I stop *crying*?'

'I could hazard a guess.'

'Don't, I'm not interested,' she cried, which was an outright lie. 'It's so *hot*!'

'Do you know what we're going to do?' Luke said forcefully. 'We'll leave a note for Caleb, take Cecilia, buy some sandwiches and fruit and go to the beach.

Your credit won't vanish at the bank if you don't work today.'

She scrubbed her eyes. 'I got lemonade all *over* you,' she hiccuped.

'I'll have a shower. We can be gone in ten minutes.'

'S—sounds like a marvellous idea.'

In many ways it was. But the beach meant swimming and swimming meant the glisten of sun on Luke's wet back as he lay face down on a towel beside Sally; she gritted her teeth and closed her eyes and tried to relax, and came painfully close to snapping at Cecilia when the child spilt sand near her mother's face.

I'm a bitch, Sally thought miserably. Wanting to yell at my kid because my hormones are acting up. Not that Luke cares—I'm wearing the same bikini I wore in St Pierre and he hasn't even looked at me.

She did not want to think about St Pierre. She got up from the sand and went for a swim by herself, ploughing between the waves with more determination than grace; and on the way home to Stellars Cove she addressed herself almost solely to Cecilia.

The next day Caleb went into town to help Luke move into his apartment, which meant Sally had to suffer through her brother's enthusiastic descriptions of Luke's stereo equipment and jacuzzi. Luke did not appear for the next two days. Sally missed him horribly, castigated herself for missing him, and when he arrived on the fourth day was furious that Cecilia ran to greet him as if he were a long-lost brother.

Or father, Sally thought, giving Luke a brief, impersonal smile and wished she could think of some way to cure her foul mood other than getting into bed with the man.

Luke gave her a shrewd look that she missed, because she was kneeling to tie Cecilia's sneaker lace. 'I'd like to take you out for dinner tonight, Sally, to celebrate surviving the move,' he said. 'Although I don't know why it should be so difficult to move one's belongings from one place to another, do you?'

'I've lived in this house all my life,' she said shortly. 'So I wouldn't know. I don't think I——'

'Please, Sal. Otherwise I shall go on a pub crawl and get thoroughly drunk.'

'I doubt whether you'd do that.'

'Think how rotten I'd feel tomorrow if I did. You wouldn't wish that on me, would you?'

She had behaved herself all week and it had brought her nothing but misery. She bit her lip. 'All right, I'll go,' she announced, much too vehemently for a simple dinner invitation.

'I'll pick you up at seven. In the meantime I'll cut the grass. Coming, Cecilia?'

Sally had made herself a very pretty figured silk dress two years ago for Caleb's graduation from junior high school. But when she looked at herself in the mirror before she left she knew that the dress had never before made her look so seductive or so feminine. She pulled a face at herself and started down the stairs.

Luke was standing in the living-room watching her descent. In his light grey summer-weight suit worn with a pale blue shirt and an elegant tie he looked so different from the man who had mowed the grass that her breath caught in her throat. She had never seen him in a suit before; nothing had quite prepared her for his air of distinction, of understated sophistication. She knew why Althea had married him.

His smile was lazy but the look in his eyes was not. 'You look very beautiful,' he said.

She had spent a full fifteen minutes on her make-up. Obviously the results were worth it. Giving him a brilliant smile and continuing her descent with a maximum rustling of her skirt, she said, 'Thank you. You look very handsome yourself.'

He took her hand and raised it to his lips. Her eyes

darkened turbulently, and for a moment they could have been naked in the darkened hotel room in St Pierre. Then Caleb came into the room carrying Cecilia. Without hurry Luke released Sally's hand and said lightly, 'Will we pass, Caleb?'

Caleb was looking at his sister, a strange expression on his face. 'Yeah,' he said slowly. 'You look great, sis.'

In a very different way Sally felt naked again, as though Caleb for the first time was seeing her as a beautiful woman. She swallowed the lump in her throat and heard Luke tease, 'Hey, what about me?'

Caleb said even more slowly, 'You look great together.'

Sally said brightly, 'Well! We'd better be going. Night, Cecilia. Sleep well, sweetheart.'

Unexpectedly Cecilia threw herself forward, clamping her arms around Sally's neck. 'I want to go, too!' she wailed.

Luke steadied Sally's elbow. 'Not tonight, Cecilia,' he said in his deep voice. 'But tomorrow we'll all go to McDonalds—my treat.'

McDonalds was Cecilia's idea of culinary perfection. She loosened her hold on Sally and blinked at Luke. 'Caleb too?'

'Everyone except Sidney. And if you like, we'll order an extra hamburger for him and bring it home with us.'

'He'd like that,' Cecilia said solemnly. 'But no tomato or lettuce in it. He thinks salad is yukky.'

'So is it a deal?' Luke asked.

'I'll have french fries, onion rings, a strawberry shake and a chocolate sundae,' Cecilia gloated.

'And I'll be in the poorhouse!' Luke joked. 'Now kiss your mother goodnight—we've got to go.'

He had spoken with an easy authority to which Cecilia instantly responded. She gave Sally a wet kiss, smearing her lipstick, and unselfconsciously held out her arms to Luke, transferring some of the lipstick to his cheek when she kissed him. Caleb took her back, and the two of them waved goodbye as Sally and Luke went out of the door.

'I've never known her to behave like that before,' Sally said. 'She doesn't usually make a fuss when I go out.'

'How often do you go out?' Luke asked drily. 'I don't think you've allowed yourself much life apart from her—she's bound to react if she thinks I'm taking you away from her.'

'You couldn't do that!' Sally replied swiftly.

He said blandly, 'I wouldn't try. Hold still, your lipstick's smudged.'

He touched the corner of her mouth with his handkerchief. She could smell the faint astringency of his shaving lotion overlying the familiar scent of his skin and fought the urge to do as Cecilia had done and throw herself into his arms. Taking the handkerchief from him, she rubbed his cheek. 'Now we're both respectable,' she said.

'I don't feel at all respectable. It's a good thing you've got all that make-up on.' He turned on the ignition and backed out of the driveway.

Sally sat very still. So he was not immune to her . . . she began to describe the history professor's latest offering, making Luke laugh outright, and started to enjoy herself. They ate at the city's newest hotel at the waterfront, the illuminated masts of the schooner *Bluenose* visible through the plate-glass windows, the notes of a piano wafting from the bar. The food was exquisitely prepared and served, and Luke knew his wines; Sally forgot all the ups and downs of the past few days and relaxed her guard. She told Luke about some of the battles she had had with her mother. She described her disastrous wedding night, on which Bruce had drunk himself to insensibility. She dug deep for the precious memories she had of her father, a handsome, light-hearted man who had dealt with her mother's iron principles by abandoning her right after Caleb was born. 'When Bruce left after Cecilia was born it seemed like history repeating itself,' she said, rotating her wine-glass so that the candlelight shot ruby sparks through the wine. 'I don't blame my father for leaving. I do blame him for not keeping in touch. I have no idea to this day what became of him.'

'The psychologists would say that in reaching out to Bruce you were looking for a father figure.'

'Some father,' she said with a wry twist of her mouth.

Luke looked at her thoughtfully; the points of the candles were shining in her eyes as she gazed into her wine glass. He said, 'Caleb's the one who's kept you from being soured on the entire male sex.'

'Caleb's a sweetheart! I don't know how I would have managed without him the last few years.'

Luke looked even more thoughtful. But all he said was, 'Are you going to tackle the dessert menu?'

'Of course! If Cecilia can have a strawberry shake and a chocolate sundae, I can surely have meringue glacé or pecan cheesecake or homemade hazelnut ice-cream with rich creamy chocolate sauce . . .'

Luke said, an odd note in his voice, 'You may have all three if you wish, my dear.'

Sally met his eyes, dropped her own in confusion, and felt a blush creep up her throat. 'Luke——'

'I just want you to have a good time,' he said gently.

She felt perilously close to tears and could not have said why. 'Tell me about *your* parents. I've talked too much.'

'No, you haven't. I have the feeling you've talked far too little over the years.'

'No one to talk to.'

'For the next four months, I'm here. You can tell me anything you like, Sal.'

His face was very serious. Can I, Luke, she wanted to say. Can I tell you I'm afraid of falling in love with you? Can I tell you that four months seems at one and the same time like a lifetime and like the blink of an eye? She said neutrally, 'You're a good listener.'

'Must go with the job,' he muttered.

'No, Luke,' she said strongly. 'It goes with you. Because you care about people.'

'People?' he questioned. 'Or is it more specific, Sal?'

Suddenly frightened, she took a gulp of wine. 'Your parents,' she ordered. 'Tell me about them.'

'What are you afraid of?' he demanded.

'Putting on ten pounds when I read the dessert menu,' she said glibly.

'Still running, Sally?'

'Your parents, Luke.'

'I like fighting with you,' he said softly. 'You don't back down . . . ah, here's the dessert menu.'

Sally swallowed the last of her wine and grabbed the menu, trying to focus on cheesecake versus meringue. When the waiter left them Luke said reflectively, as if he had never mentioned the word running, 'My parents had a wonderful marriage, full of humour, laced with conflict, fortified by love—I probably placed too many expectations on Althea as a result. But my mother died when I was thirteen. My father was devastated, and never really recovered. He had a fatal heart attack five years later.'

'You must have been lonely.'

'Probably why I married young. But it wasn't fair of me to invest Althea with all my mother's virtues.'

Sally said pungently, 'It wasn't fair of Althea to have affairs with two other men.'

'You wouldn't do that, Sally.'

She managed a weak smile. 'Where would I find the time? Talking about time, I shouldn't be too late home tonight—I have to work tomorrow.'

'I thought we might drop by the apartment on the way home—I'd like you to see it. No ulterior motives, I promise.'

Sally had her fair share of curiosity about Luke's apartment; and the wine had given her a false bravado. 'I trust you,' she said airily, forgetting to question whether she could trust herself. 'I'd love to see your apartment. Caleb was very impressed with it.'

Luke was renting a condominium downtown, its living-room windows overlooked the harbour. 'I got a good price on it because it's to be sold at the beginning of the year,' he said as he ushered Sally into the entrance hall.

If this was another reminder of the temporary nature of his stay, she ignored it. Instead she admired the hand-woven rug placed over the flagstone flooring, and the misty colours of the watercolour on the end wall. There were more paintings in the living-room, and a ceiling-to-floor granite fireplace; the bathroom with its diffuse lighting, its royal blue ceramic tiles and its flourishing rubber plants delighted her. He showed her the den, set up as a businesslike office, and the ultramodern kitchen; although it was a miracle of technology, she preferred the muddle of her own. And then she was walking into his bedroom. 'I haven't finished unpacking in here yet,' Luke said.

In one lightning-swift glance Sally saw packing boxes, pine furniture, and the double bed, covered with a forest-green spread. She whirled, knowing she had to get out of here, crashed into Luke's chest and threw her arms around him, making an inarticulate sound in her throat. He seized her, almost lifting her off her feet, and began kissing her, rough, hungry kisses which she matched with a frantic hunger all of her own. Then he did lift her off her feet. They fell on the bed, Luke fumbling with the fastenings of her dress as she kicked off her shoes.

Afterwards Sally never quite remembered how they got out of their clothes, although Luke's suit was flung to the floor with less ceremony than it deserved. She did remember the glorious certainty of their bodies naked on the bed. She remembered Luke's hands searching the sensitivities of her flesh, his avid mouth roaming her body, his voice hoarse with desire, her own voice pleading with him to take her, take her, take her . . .

Take her he did, in a lovemaking as elemental as a hurricane and as fierce as a forest fire; and when it was all over, they lay entwined and exhausted on the bed. Sally felt as the forest must feel when the hurricane has passed, the boughs subsiding to a singing stillness, the diamond droplets of rain absorbed into the measureless sky. Peace was in her heart, surpassing the memory of tumult and the piercing beauty of their union: a peace that did not need words; a peace that was beyond love.

But Luke shattered that peace. In a sudden violent movement he pulled away from her. Sitting on the edge of the bed, his head in his hands, he muttered, 'God, Sally, I've done it again—I swore I wouldn't touch you, that you could trust me. I should never have brought you here.'

She fought the lethargy of her limbs and the slowness of her brain. Propping herself on one arm, her body a taut graceful curve, she said, 'Luke, you mustn't apologise. I'm as much responsible as——'

'I promised!' he said hoarsely. 'We should never have made love. But it won't happen again, I swear it won't.' He ran his fingers through his hair, looking at the scattered clothes on the floor as though he wasn't sure whose they were or how they had got there. As if the words were forced from him he said harshly, 'Do you know what the worst thing is? I couldn't help myself—I was totally out of control. I never felt like that with Althea.'

She had never felt like that with Bruce, either. 'But, Luke——'

'A platonic relationship—that's what I figured we could have.' He was looking at her as if he hated her, his eyes whirlpools of blue. 'Platonic—that's a joke!'

'But, Luke——'

'I'm caught in a goddamned trap,' he muttered, and dropped his head to his hands again.

But Luke, but Luke, but Luke . . . she sounded like a record caught in the groove, Sally thought numbly, and heard him say in a voice empty of all emotion, 'I'll get dressed and take you home.'

She watched him stoop to pick up his clothes and then walk out of the room; she heard the bathroom door close behind him. She remembered the thick, obscuring mists of St Pierre and felt them swirl around her now, congealing her blood, turning her heart to stone.

CHAPTER ELEVEN

ALL of her movements calling for an immense effort of will, Sally began to get dressed, for she could not bear Luke to return to the bedroom to find her naked. The fastenings on her dress had never seemed so complicated; she had not known there existed such loneliness as she felt when Luke came back into the room and said briefly, 'Are you ready to go?'

She nodded, not trusting her voice, and picked up her bag from the floor. They left the apartment, stood like two strangers in the elevator, and did not speak on the drive home. Sally had her seat-belt unfastened almost before the car came to a halt. She scrambled out, praying that Caleb would not have waited up for her, and said breathlessly, 'Goodnight, Luke.'

'Wait, Sally!' He leaned across the seat. 'I told Cecilia we'd all go to McDonalds tomorrow. I don't want to break that promise as well.'

'Maybe I'll break a leg between now and then,' Sally said grimly. 'That way I won't have to go.'

'You'll spoil it for her if you don't go.'

That he was telling the truth did not improve Sally's temper. 'And what time will this delightful dinner party occur?'

'I'll get here at five.'

'Fine,' she said. 'Goodnight,' and slammed the car door.

Caleb had not waited up for her. She went to her room, hung up the dress in the very back of her cupbard, a difficult job because her eyes were blinded by tears, went to bed and cried herself to sleep.

Unfortunately, when she got up in the morning she looked exactly like a woman who had cried herself to sleep. Cold water on her face followed by a hot bath did very little to help; Caleb's comment was, 'You look like Sidney when the dog next door took his bone. You sick?'

Sally thought of various replies, censored a couple of them, and said economically, 'Luke and I had a fight.'

'What about?'

'Don't ask.'

'Are you in love with him?' Caleb helped himself to cornflakes.

'No! I can hear Cecilia coming, change the subject, Caleb.'

His hand resting on the sugar bowl, Caleb said, 'I think you do love him. You're not being self-sacrificing because of Cecilia and me, are you? Figuring you've got to stay single until the two of us are launched into the world?'

'Luke has never suggested I be anything other than single,' Sally snaped, and then could have bitten off her tongue. She heard the pad of Cecilia's bare feet on the living-room floor and called, 'We're in the kitchen, hon,' adding quickly, 'Luke's promised Cecilia a trip to McDonalds tonight, but after that I don't think I'll be seeing him again. So please don't talk about him any more, Caleb.' She broke off abruptly, because her voice was trembling.

'I hate seeing you upset!'

'What's upset, Mum?' Cecilia asked; she was still in her long nightgown, trailing her teddy bear in one hand.

'I didn't sleep well, love, that's all,' Sally said evasively, bending to hug her daughter. 'Mmm, you're lovely and warm. Want some waffles for breakfast?'

Cecilia hoisted herself up to the table. 'We're going to McDonalds tonight.'

'That's right,' Sally said steadily. 'You could wear your new green trousers.'

'I love McDonalds,' Cecilia announced. 'I love Luke, too. Can I have the cornflakes, Caleb?'

Sally turned away to plug in the waffle-iron. If she stopped seeing Luke Cecilia would be hurt, Caleb would be angry, and Neville and Maria would be full of questions. Not to mention her own feelings.

Caleb was getting ready for work, packing himself some sandwiches for lunch. 'I might be home early today,' he said as he went out of the door. 'I'm painting at the Michaelsons—there's not much left to do.'

'Be home by five, anyway,' Sally replied. 'I need your moral support.'

He gave her one of his clumsy hugs. 'Take it easy today, sis.'

Cecilia finished breakfast and started organising a dolls' tea party, chattering away to herself. Sally began to work. At ten thirty Lynette arrived. 'Coffee-break,' she announced, plunking herself down at the kitchen table. 'Where's Cecilia?'

'Upstairs tidying her bedroom. Which means it ends up in a worse muddle than when she started.'

Lynette gave a snort of laughter. 'She and I have quite a bit in common. You don't look so hot, Sally—anything wrong?'

Lynette, for all her flippancy, could be trusted to be discreet. 'Luke and I made love last night,' Sally said miserably.

'That's supposed to make you feel better, not worse.'

'Well, it wasn't really making love. Lust would be more like it.' Trying to concentrate on what she was doing, Sally put coffee in the filter.

'Nothing wrong with that every now and then.'

'He apologised afterwards. Said it would never happen again.' Two tears dripped on to the coffee. 'He doesn't love me, Lynette . . . he only wants to go to bed with me. I felt used. Thrown aside. Oh damn, why does everything I say sound like a cliché?'

Lynette got up swiftly, moved the coffee-pot out of reach and put her arms around her friend. 'You want him to love you?'

'*I* don't know,' Sally cried. 'I'm so confused!'

'He's not the type who's out for a one-night stand,' Lynette said forthrightly. 'I've met a few of those, and Luke Sheridan isn't one of them.'

'No. He's out for a four-month stand,' Sally said bitterly.

'Maybe he just needs more time,' Lynette suggested.

'For what?' Sally wiped her eyes.

'To discover that he loves you. You told me he's divorced, maybe he needs a while to recover. *You* should understand that.' Lynette reached over for the box of Kleenex on the table. 'I know one thing for sure—he cares about you.'

'Oh, he *likes* me.'

'That's not a bad beginning. He's certainly not using you, Sally.'

'You sound very wise all of a sudden,' Sally said suspiciously.

Lynette laughed. 'It's always easier to sort out someone else's problems rather than your own. I met this absolute *hunk* at the yacht club on Saturday night, but I'm supposed to be going steady with John, and then Roger—remember him? The oil painter?—he's coming to town at the end of September, and what am I going to do with them all?' Lynette fluttered her lashes complacently.

'*I'll* never have an affair again!' Sally proclaimed.

'Don't be silly—Luke's much more masculine than Dennis and much more mature than Bruce and much more reliable than your father. Deny it.'

'I can't. He's wonderful,' Sally said helplessly.

Lynette looked even more complacent after this

admission. 'Coffee,' she said firmly. 'If Luke hasn't proposed by Christmas, I'll go and see him myself.'

'Don't you dare!' Sally exclaimed, looking as fierce as Tigger the cat when Sidney got too close to her feed bowl.

'I'm sure I won't have to,' Lynette said lightly. 'Plug in the kettle, Sally.'

Feeling better for having shared her burden, Sally did as she was told.

Sally was to remember Lynette's words about Luke's theoretical proposal later that day. About three o'clock she finished the final section that the history professor had given her; needing some physical activity, she decided to clean out the garden shed, and soon she and Cecilia were coated with dust and cobwebs. Then Lynette arrived. She looked at Sally's smudged face with amusement. 'Can I borrow Cecilia for a while? I've got some new finger paints that I thought she might like to try out.'

Cecilia, naturally, was agreeable, and Sally went back to sorting out nails. The tidily arranged tools and the neat rows of bottles on the shelves were soothing to her bruised spirits. She had cleaned the windows and was sweeping the floor when she heard a car drive up: Lynette, bringing Cecilia home in the car, she decided; Lynette was not as fond of walking as Sally. But simultaneously she heard footsteps on the road and Caleb's voice call out, 'Hi there, Luke! Nice day, eh?'

Luke. He was early. Sally stood rooted to the spot, clutching the broom, frightened of seeing him again, certainly not anxious to appear in her oldest clothes with cobwebs in her hair. The car door slammed. Luke said easily, 'Wonderful. All set to dine out tonight?'

'Yeah,' Caleb replied; he sounded much closer to the shed. 'You did say the Sheraton, didn't you?'

Luke laughed. 'I did not!'

When Caleb spoke again, his voice had deepened a notch. 'Listen, Luke, before we go in to the house, there's something I'd like to ask you.'

'Oh? What's that?'

Luke's voice was closer too. Although the shed door was slightly ajar, Sally could not see either of them. She had several choices. She could drop a bottle of nails to alert them to her presence, she could waltz out of the door smiling brightly, or she could stay where she was. She decided to stay where she was.

Without preamble Caleb said, 'I don't know what's going on between you and Sally, but she was upset today—I don't want to see her get hurt again, Luke.'

Sally winced, wishing she had dropped the bottle of nails. But it was too late now. There was a pause before Luke said quietly, 'It is not my intention to hurt Sally.'

'What are your intentions?' Caleb said bluntly. 'You planning on marrying my sister?'

'No,' said Luke in a peculiar voice.

Stabbed to the heart, Sally stood still. I've been fooling myself, she thought dazedly. I've been fooling myself for weeks. I'm not afraid of falling in love with Luke. I *am* in love with him. But he doesn't want to marry me . . .

'Isn't she good enough for you?' Caleb said belligerently.

'She's too good for me.'

'Then why won't you marry her?'

'She's not in love with me, Caleb,' Luke said patiently. 'She made it very clear to me that she didn't want commitment or even emotional involvement.'

'Didn't look like that to me this morning—she'd been crying. Sally doesn't cry very often and when she does it doesn't mean she's not involved. If you see what I mean.'

There was a trace of amusement in Luke's voice. 'I do see. So your suggestion is that I ask her to marry me?'

'She probably will.'

'I just don't want you hanging around for as long as it suits you and then taking off,' Caleb said violently. 'Bruce did that to her. And Dad did, too, years ago. Two's enough. She doesn't need a third.'

'I may have to go back to New Brunswick after Christmas.'

'Sally could go to New Brunswick. I finish school in June and then I'm on my own.'

Another pregnant pause. 'So you think I should ask her to marry me?' Luke asked in the same peculiar voice.

'Yeah. She deserves to be happy. She's been as good to me as anyone could be.'

'Yes, she deserves to be happy.' A small silence. 'Anything else, Caleb?'

'No. I reckon I said all I wanted to. We'd better go in, she'll be wondering what we're doing out here.'

Sally heard their steps retreat, and then the front door open and close. She sneaked out of the shed, skulking behind it, then made a dash for the road. Ducking behind some bushes she began to walk in the direction of Lynette's, the general idea being to deceive Luke and Caleb into thinking she had been gone when they arrived. Although she was acting with some degree of intelligence, her feelings were less easy to categorise. Outrage and pain were certainly among them. Outrage that Caleb and Luke should discuss her future, pain that Luke should have to be cajoled into marriage. But under those emotions lay another: pure wonderment, for she loved a man, and surely love was an immeasurable gift.

Five minutes later she met Lynette and Cecilia walking hand in hand in her direction. 'Are we late?' Lynette called.

'No. I just thought I'd walk up to meet you,' Sally said breathlessly.

Cecilia, who was generously spattered with finger paint, said, 'We had fun, Mum. Is Luke there yet?'

'Why don't we go and see?' said Sally, ashamed that she should even so indirectly deceive her daughter. She feigned surprise when she saw Luke's car parked outside the house, saw Lynette's raised brows and bluffed, 'I'm such a mess—I hate Luke to see me like this.'

Lynette understood this kind of reasoning. 'I'll distract him while you sneak upstairs and change.'

Luke and Caleb were in the kitchen; Lynette took Sally's Technicoloured daughter in there too, and Sally ran for her bedroom. At least now neither Luke nor Caleb would know she had been cleaning the shed. After changing into red overalls with a red and white knitted shirt, she went downstairs. Everyone was still in the kitchen. She said casually, 'Hello, all,' then rolled her eyes in her head in mock horror at the sight of her daughter. 'Some day we must get Lynette to teach you that the paint is supposed to go on the paper,' she said amiably. 'C'mon, sweetie, clean clothes for McDonalds. Lynette, why don't you come into town with us?'

Lynette shook her head. 'Family outing. Besides, I hate hamburgers.'

'They've got chicken and you're family. Do come.'

Again Lynette raised her eyebrows, a gesture she performed with flair. 'OK,' she said, 'on condition you'll drop me off at home on the way back.'

'Great! Come along, Cecilia—green trousers and a clean shirt.'

Cecilia was perfectly agreeable to changing, and Sally got out of the kitchen without having to talk to Luke. Lynette would act as a buffer, she thought, one more person between herself and Luke. When they all went outside she got in the back of the car with Cecilia and Lynette, and at McDonalds she sat as far from Luke as she could. She had no intention of spoiling the outing for her daughter; she chatted and laughed so vivaciously that she was the life of the party, all without exchanging a dozen direct words with Luke. She scuttled into the back seat for the drive home, and tried to persuade Lynette to come in for coffee. But Lynette refused, and once the rest of them were in the house Caleb said guilelessly, 'I'll bath Cecilia and get her ready for bed, Sally, so you and Luke can have a visit.'

Her back to Luke, Sally scowled malevolently at her brother. But Caleb merely smiled, picked up his niece and headed upstairs, where he turned on the bathwater to its fullest volume and shut the bathroom door with aggressive firmness. Luke said evenly, 'What the hell's the matter with you tonight, Sally?'

She gave him the glittering smile she had been producing all evening. 'After such a gourmet feast, what could possibly be the matter?'

She was standing by the picture window, as far from him as she could be. He said tightly, 'You've been avoiding me all evening.'

'There were three other people there, Luke—you surely didn't expect me to devote myself to you?'

'It's not like you to be bitchy.' His eyes narrowed. 'What's wrong?'

She made a little pirouette, a poor imitation of Neville's. 'It was very kind of you to treat us all—a nice ending to the summer.'

'Sally, will you for God's sake stand still!' he exploded.

Her hands on her hips, she glared at him across the coffee-table. '*I* should be asking what's wrong with *you*,' she retorted. 'Or are you always this rude when you eat hamburgers?'

He glared back at her. 'If you'd stand still long enough and stop making smart remarks, I'd be asking you to marry me.'

In unwitting obedience Sally stood still, her face

white with shock. She sputtered, 'If this is some kind of joke, I don't think it's very funny.'

'It's no joke. I mean it.'

He did. Her mouth suddenly dry, Sally exclaimed, 'You don't want to marry me!'

His smile broke through the grim purpose in his face. 'I wouldn't be asking you if I didn't.'

'Yes, you would,' she retorted. 'You're just doing what Caleb told you to.'

Luke hesitated a fraction too long. 'What are you talking about?'

'I overheard you. I was in the shed.'

Upstairs the pipes clanked as they always did when the bathwater was turned off. *You planning on marrying my sister?* Caleb had asked. *No*, Luke had replied; and the pain of that denial had been with Sally ever since, buried under her vivacity, causing the dead weight of exhaustion she felt now.

'I see,' Luke said slowly. 'If you overheard us, then you must realise I've changed my mind since then.'

'Sure,' she said tartly. 'At five o'clock you don't want to marry me, at eight o'clock you do. That doesn't seem like much of a basis for marriage.'

He leaned forward. 'Sally, I genuinely thought you didn't want marriage. When Caleb told me you were upset last night . . . it caused me to wonder if *you* hadn't changed your mind.'

Tell me you love me, one little part of her brain screamed. 'Well, I haven't,' she said, and from somewhere the words came tumbling out. 'I was married once before. It was not my happiest eight months. Once married, twice shy, and I'm not at all sure that love and marriage go together like a horse and carriage—if the horse bolts, the carriage gets smashed up.'

Her fists were clenched at her sides and her jaw jutted defiantly. 'Sally, I can only say that when Caleb suggested I marry you, it seemed a good idea to me. It seemed to fit . . . as though we belong together.'

'No.'

'We belong together in bed.'

She flushed, staring down at the magazines on the coffee-table. 'That's different. Anyway, I don't want to do that any more.'

He took a step closer. 'You're lying,' he said. 'You want me as badly as I want you. I've never wanted a woman as I want you, Sally.'

Tell me you love me. 'Luke, I will not have you and Caleb arranging my life for me, no matter how nice both of you think it would be if I married you.' Her voice rose. 'Caleb wouldn't have to worry about me any more, one less stray in the world, and you'd have instantly available sex, all very convenient. But I will not——'

The doorbell rang. Sally broke off in mid-sentence; she had been yelling at Luke like a fishwife. 'Excuse me,' she muttered, and ran for the door.

A very large policeman stood on the step. His patrol car was parked next to Luke's sedan. 'I'm looking for Sally Cowan,' he said.

She felt a flash of gratitude that Cecilia, Caleb and Luke were all safely in the house; otherwise she would probably have fainted on the spot. 'I'm Sally Cowan. Please come in.'

The policeman followed her indoors, taking off his cap. He had a ruddy face with such a non-committal expression on it that Sally was certain he had overheard her remark about instantly available sex. He said formally, 'I understand Neville Bartlett spends quite a bit of time here. Anything you could tell me about his whereabouts the last twenty-four hours would be helpful.'

'Is he all right?' Sally demanded. The policeman nodded. 'Then why are you asking?'

'There's been an—er, episode at the church.'

Wondering if she were in the grip of a more than usually illogical dream, Sally repeated, 'Episode?'

'Take a look at the steeple out of your window, ma'am.'

Sally and Luke went to the picture window. The pretty little church was on the other side of the cove. Puzzled, Sally said. 'There's something on top of the steeple.'

'The minister's chair. With a sign tacked to the seat saying *God is not Dead*.'

Sally felt a bubble of laughter rise in her chest and hastily smothered it as the policeman said heavily, 'Public mischief, ma'am.'

It was exactly the sort of thing Neville would do; and he was definitely agile enough to scale the steeple. In a businesslike tone Sally relayed what she knew of Neville's movements and finished firmly, 'As far as I know, the rest of the time he was home.'

The policeman had jotted down a couple of notes in his book. 'Thank you, ma'am,' he said, carefully replaced his cap, and allowed her to usher him out of the door. She waited until the patrol car had driven away before saying, 'I bet Neville did it.'

'I bet he did, too,' Luke rejoined. 'He'll probably get away with it, though, because I'm sure he's smart enough to have covered his tracks. Which leaves me to wonder what he'll try next.'

Wishing she did not agree so implicitly with everything Luke had said, Sally vowed, 'I'll give him a good lecture the next time I see him.'

'I'm not sure lectures have much effect on young men like Neville.' Luke took Sally by the elbow. 'But that's another reason you should marry me—I could take Neville in hand.'

Tell me you love me. 'No, Luke, I won't marry you,' Sally said evenly. 'And now I'd really prefer you to leave before Cecilia comes downstairs again.'

'Cecilia likes me. So does Caleb.'

'And think how much better off I'd be financially—you haven't mentioned that,' Sally retorted. She rubbed her forehead with the back of her hand, feeling as though she were an actress who had been given some very bad lines in a scene that had neve quite touched reality. 'I'm going up to read Cecilia her story. I'd like you to be gone when I come downstairs.'

Luke took her by the arm, the grim lines back around his mouth. 'I haven't handled this well. I didn't mean——'

The bathroom door opened so she could hear Cecilia's clear treble and Caleb's deeper tones. 'I've got to go,' she said in a furious whisper, and tore herself free. She ran for the stairs, not looking back.

When she came downstairs fifteen minutes later the living-room was empty, and to Caleb's query about Luke's whereabouts, she responded brusquely, 'He's gone. He asked me to marry him and I said no.'

Surprise and chagrin chased themselves across Caleb's face. 'He did? And you said *no*? Why? What's wrong with you, Sally?'

It was the second time that day she had been asked what was wrong with her. 'In his lists of reasons why I should be so terribly grateful to marry him he mentioned sex, money, Cecilia, you and Neville. But do you know what he left out?' She paused with unconscious histrionic effect. 'Love. He never once mentioned the word love. He likes me, he feels sorry for me, he thinks I'm a gallant little woman who's struggling against tremendous odds, and he lusts after me. But he doesn't love me. So that's that.'

'Sure he does.' But Caleb did not sound convinced.

'No, he doesn't. I was in the shed when you were talking to him—*you* gave him the idea of proposing marriage.'

Consternation was now the predominant expression on Caleb's face. 'You heard us?'

'I did. And if you interfere again, no matter how well-meaning you are, I'll cut you up in little bits and sell you as lobster bait!'

Had her voice not quivered Caleb might have laughed. Instead he put his arms around his sister and said sincerely, 'I'm sorry, Sally . . . but if I know Luke, he'll be back. 'I'm sure he loves you—how could he help it?'

CHAPTER TWELVE

LUKE did not come back. Sally ached for him, wept for him, raged against him and somehow kept her tangled emotions to herself. She produced a poster and a form letter for an amateur theatrical group, typed some student essays, played with Cecilia, lectured Neville and cooked three meals a day, and began to discover that one does not die of unrequited love: one merely feels as if life has lost all its savour. She was not short-tempered with any of her various dependants; she did not cry in front of anyone. But she did not laugh either. And she never mentioned Luke's name.

Three days passed in this fashion, and each felt as long as a week. On the third evening Sally went for a long walk by herself, leaving Caleb at home with Cecilia. She clambered along the rocky shoreline, her only companions the gulls and cormorants, her eyes returning again and again to the horizon, where the confines of the harbour gave way to the vast expanse of open Atlantic. Love should free her in the same way, she thought miserably. It should free her spirit to soar with the white-winged gulls, and liberate her from the loneliness of their mournful cries against the orange-washed sky. But it had not done so.

Shivering, for the wind held the first sharpness of autumn, she turned around and went home. The glow of light from the windows of her house gave her the first peace she had known all day; she hurried indoors and knew instantly that the house was empty.

There was a note on the kitchen table, a phone number at the top, then a scrawl of words in Caleb's normally tidy handwriting:

> Neville has a bet on that he can pick up some drugs
> at one of the clubs on Dow Street. I've gone to bring
> him home. Cecilia at Lynette's. Love, Caleb.

Dow Street had the worst reputation of any street in
the city; Sally would not have walked on it alone after
dark, and it was certainly no place for a fourteen-year-
old boy bent on mischief. Nor was it the place for Caleb,
who despite broad shoulders and lessons in self-
defence cherished a certain naïve belief in the essential
goodness of his fellow man. Dow Street did not
encourage brotherly love.

She read the note again, feeling the cold grip of fear;
and knew exactly what she was going to do. Without
stopping to think she called a cab, then rang
information and was given Luke's number. Quickly she
dialled it, praying that he was home, knowing that she
needed him and would turn to him before anyone else.
When he answered on the third ring she was so
overcome by relief that it took her a moment to find her
voice.

'Hello?' he repeated sharply.

'Luke, it's Sally.'

'Sally! I'm so glad you phoned back, I wasn't sure
you would.'

'Phone back? I don't——'

'I left my number with Caleb. Didn't you get the
message?'

She suddenly realised that the number at the top of
the note was the number she had just dialled. 'So he
told you what's happened?'

'I don't understand . . .'

'About Neville and the drugs!'

'Sally, we'd better start all over again. Why are you
calling me?'

She tamped down panic and swiftly relayed Caleb's

note. 'The cab's just arrived so I'm heading down there now. Will you meet me there? I'm scared to be alone.'

'Go to the corner of Dow and Canning. I'll be waiting for you. And don't worry—we'll find him.'

Not stopping to ask him why he had phoned, she said goodbye, grabbed her wallet and a jacket and ran outdoors. When the cab driver looked doubtful about her choice of destination, she said rapidly, 'It's OK—a friend's meeting me there,' and realised gratefully that Luke had not attempted to dissuade her from going. She realised something else in an uprush of happiness that pierced her to the core: that in a few minutes she would be seeing him again.

Because it was Friday night Dow Street was crowded. Sally paid the driver and got out on the corner of Canning and Dow. An old man in a filthy tweed jacket stumbled past her, muttering to himself; two smartly dressed black girls eyed him contemptuously as they stalked past on three-inch heels. Rock music blared from the nearest tavern as a red-haired man pushed through the swing door. Swaying a little, he yelled at Sally, 'Hey, babe, you waitin' for someone?'

'Yes,' said Luke, 'for me,' and took Sally by the arm.

The red-haired man grinned foolishly and beat a retreat into the tavern. Sally did not blame him, for in faded jeans and a black T-shirt Luke looked formidable. She tried to banish a smile that must have been every bit as foolish as the red-haired man's, and said intelligently, 'Hello, Luke.'

His sea-blue eyes fastened themselves on her face, discerning the anxiety beneath the smile. 'It's OK, Sally, we're going to find them,' he said.

Unconsciously she wrapped her fingers around his wrist. 'We've got to!'

'We will.' He patted her sleeve. 'We'll start up this side of the street checking out the bars, asking if anyone's seen them. Come on.'

The next hour widened Sally's horizons, not necessarily in directions she would have chosen, as a parade of derelicts, prostitutes and street-wise kids passed in front of her. She held tightly to Luke. Something in his bearing caused the crowds to part around them; although he was never anything but polite, obscenities had a tendency to die half-spoken. But no one he asked had seen Caleb or Neville.

They went from a tavern that was hazy with smoke and reeked of hot grease to a gloomy little club with a black-painted stage on which two scantily clad dancers circled lethargically. The comments of the audience made Sally more uncomfortable than the dancers, whose techniques Neville undoubtedly would have scorned. They circled a hall full of pinball machines and androgynous young people in black leather and chains, whose turquoise and orange hairdos Cecilia would have enjoyed. They did not see Neville buying drugs from any of a number of likely prospects, nor did they see Caleb trying to stop him. As dingy building after dingy building yielded no clues, Sally felt fear begin to close in on her. Luke said calmly, 'Don't panic, Sal. Dow Street is only so big, sooner or later we'll find them.'

'I'd be much more scared if you weren't with me,' she gulped.

He gave her a quick, hard kiss, which briefly transformed Dow Street into somewhere quite different. Then he suddenly turned his head, his face intent. 'What's that?'

She heard the sound of a scuffle and a bitten-off cry. Then a voice bellowed, 'You stop that!'

'Stay here!' Luke ordered, and plunged into the darkness between a video shop and a movie theatre.

Sally plunged after him, adrenalin banishing her fears, because she had recognised the voice as Caleb's. A flashlight appeared in Luke's hand. He switched it

on, and in the beam of light she saw Neville splayed
against a brick wall, squirming in the grip of a man in a
blue-checked shirt, and Caleb, half-crouched, trying to
hold off two more men, one of whom outweighed him
by a hundred pounds.

Luke said in a voice Ross Deighton would have
recognised, 'You guys have got exactly one minute to
get out of here.'

He was balancing on his toes; the T-shirt showed to
full advantage the breadth of his shoulders and the
muscle-ridged chest. For a moment the tableau was
frozen like a film frame. Then the man in the blue-
checked shirt flung Neville away from him and melted
into the shadows of the alley. Caleb landed a punch on
the lighter of his attackers that propelled the man in the
same direction, and the fat man suddenly seemed to
realise he was being abandoned.

He scuttled sideways, keeping out of Luke's range,
and gave his partner another shove. In considerably
less than a minute Neville and Caleb had the brick wall
to themselves.

Caleb straightened; he was breathing hard. 'How
come I couldn't do that?' he gasped. 'They didn't pay
any attention to me when *I* yelled at them.'

'Takes a lot of practice,' Luke said in a deadpan voice.
'Are you hurt?'

Caleb swiped at his chin. 'No. But they sure weren't
fighting by the rules—good thing you came along.'

'Dow Street isn't a karate class,' Luke said grimly. He
favoured Neville with a basilisk stare. 'I hope you're
happy with the results of your bet.'

'I didn't figure it would lead to a fight,' Neville said
defensively.

'Didn't you?' Luke said sarcastically. 'Perhaps it's
time you looked a little more closely at the potential
consquences of your actions.'

'But——'

Luke overrode him, his voice with the cutting edge of a steel blade. 'If I hadn't arrived, those two guys would have used Caleb as a punching-bag right in front of your eyes. Would you have enjoyed that?'

'Of course not!' Neville said hotly.

'And had I not been home when Sally phoned, she would have come down here by herself to look for you. Is that what you wanted—Sally wandering alone along Dow Street?'

As Neville looked from Luke to Sally, all the energy seemed to drain from his body. He sagged gracelessly against the wall; it was the only time Sally had ever seen him move with anything less than elegance. 'No,' he said in a low voice.

But Luke was not through with him. 'Your stupid little prank could have caused serious harm to two people who have been nothing but good to you. I suppose we should be grateful you didn't involve Cecilia.'

'Luke——' Sally protested.

Luke did not even look at her; his gaze held Neville impaled to the wall. He said harshly, 'I love Sally more than anyone else in the world, Neville, and if you'd been even indirectly responsible for harming her, I'd have hounded you to the ends of the earth.'

Sally said blankly, 'You don't!'

Luke transferred furious blue eyes to her. 'Of course I do,' he said shortly. 'Why do you think I asked you to marry me?'

Angrily she ticked off the reasons. 'Sex, money, and so you could keep your eye on Neville!'

Some of the fury eased from his face. 'At which I would seem to be doing a lousy job.' He directed his attention back to the boy, who had visibly wilted, and said more calmly, 'You'd better decide what you're going to do with your life, Neville—dance or act the fool. If it's the latter you want, then I would suggest that you do not involve Caleb or Sally. Not if you value living.'

Very slowly Neville straightened, as if a puppet master were pulling his strings, raising him from boneless collapse to the surety of motion. He said with absolute conviction, 'I want to dance.'

Luke's answer was equally a pledge. 'Then I'll help you any way I can,' he said, holding out his hand. Neville stretched out his own and shook it.

Sally let out her pent-up breath and said in deliberate anticlimax, 'Caleb, you're going to have a black eye.'

'I'll put some ice on it,' Caleb promised, and added, 'I'll take a couple more lessons in self-defence, too. The teacher'll only have to look at my face to know why I need them.'

'We'd better go home,' she suggested; she had had enough of Dow Street. 'Cecilia's still at Lynette's.'

'And you and I have some unfinished business,' Luke said jauntily; he looked very pleased with himself.

She glanced around the ugly little alley. 'You certainly chose quite a place to start it.'

He flexed his muscles. 'Once we get rid of this crew I'm going to ask you to marry me. And I promise I'll do it differently this time.'

'You'd better be careful,' she warned. 'I might say yes. In the meantime can we please go home?'

They walked the length of Dow Street to Luke's car. The drive home was accomplished largely in silence, four people absorbed in their separate thoughts, among which Sally's, at least, were in chaos. Lynette had put Cecilia to bed at her house, Caleb invited himself there too, ostensibly so that he could bring Cecilia home in the morning, and Neville was deposited at the end of his parents' driveway. As he got out of the car the boy said, 'Sally, I appreciate you coming after me—you won't ever have to do that again. Goodnight, Luke. Thanks.' Irrepressibly he did four swirling dance steps, grinned at them impartially and ran down the path.

'I think he's learned his lesson,' Luke said. He put the car in reverse. 'Do you realise, Sally Cowan, that we have the whole house to ourselves for at least eight hours?'

She looked over at his strong profile, loving him so much that she was amazed her voice sounded so natural. 'You've got a lot of explaining to do,' she said severely.

'I know I have. That's the reason I phoned you in the first place. But before I start, *will* you marry me, Sally? For just one reason—because I love you.'

'Yes,' she said.

He stalled the car. 'You *will*?'

She could feel happiness bubbling up in her like champagne, and because she knew she was safe she said archly, 'Changed your mind already?'

'God, no!' He tried to start the car, ground the starter and said with a comical air of dismay, 'I'm useless—can't function at all. Sally, let's go home and we can talk there.'

'The first step is to start the car.'

'How can I concentrate when you smile at me like that?' He jammed his foot on the brake and kissed her with a passion she gloried in, after which he successfully backed out of the driveway. At the house Sidney greeted them as if they had been gone for weeks and he had been starved in the interim; the cats did not deign to wake up. Sally let the dog out and closed the front door. Luke said peremptorily, 'Kiss me.'

Willingly she went into his arms, from which she emerged several minutes later with her hair tousled, her cheeks scarlet and her eyes brilliant.

'Oh God, Sally, I love you,' Luke groaned. 'I'm sorry it took me so long to tell you so—when you said no to my proposal of marriage and I went home to the empty apartment, I felt totally lost. Couldn't figure out what was wrong with me. It was only today that I came to my senses and admitted something I've known subconsciously for weeks—that I'm deeply in love with you. Hit me like a ton of bricks, I might as well tell you. Give me a six-foot convict brandishing a steel pipe any day of the week over a beautiful redhead with big grey eyes.' His smile was ironic. 'We've talked a lot since we met, haven't we, Sal? But the one word we've never mentioned is love . . . I have a feeling I started to fall in love with you when you marched into my cabin and told me to move to the crew's quarters, but I had such a guard up it took me until now to figure it out.' He finished with a humility that touched her, 'Do you think you'll grow to love me, Sal?'

'I love you now,' she said. 'I've been fooling myself, too. The reason I ran away from St Pierre—or so I told myself—was I was afraid of falling in love with you. I know now I already had. But I was scared to admit it.'

Luke took her in his arms again. 'I never thought you'd love me,' he muttered, kissing her in between his words. 'I thought after all that had happened, you were off men for life.' He raised his head. 'Tell me again.'

She said proudly, 'Luke, I love you.'

'You realise I may ask you to repeat that at hourly intervals for the rest of my life?'

She ran her nails down the ridged muscles of his belly. 'Actions can speak louder than words.'

He laughed, hugged her fiercely, kissed her again and said, 'Before I left for St Pierre I had an argument with my boss. Take a woman to St Pierre, he said. No thanks, I replied, I'm off women. No affairs for me. And then you turned up to share my cabin. Fiery-tempered. Innocent as a daisy. Half-naked in that nightdress. A mass of contradictions who aroused just as many contradictions in me. How the hell was I supposed to fathom you when I couldn't understand myself? All I know is that when I went back to that empty hotel room in St Pierre I felt as if I'd been punched in the gut, and when I went to Sydney and found out you'd lied to me, kicked in the ribs into the bargain. I'd lost you. You couldn't have made it clearer that you didn't want anything more to do with me . . . so you can understand why I was a touch irate the day I came across you in the Public Gardens. It wasn't until I got home that I realised I was also blazingly happy and that I had to see you again. When you wouldn't pick up on our affair where we'd left off—another blow to my pride—I figured we could at least have a platonic relationship. Well, we both know how long that lasted.'

Her smile ruefully acknowledged the truth of his words. 'I was happy to see you, too. So happy that it terrified me.' She bit her lip. 'I had this deep irrational fear of falling in love and being abandoned, whether it was after a week in St Pierre or four months in Halifax. So I ran away before it could happen.'

'Four months is nowhere near long enough for me to show you how much I love you,' Luke said huskily, running his fingers through her tangled red curls. 'I'm not sure a lifetime will be long enough.'

'We could try.'

'Definitely.' He drew her closer. 'Sally, I understand now why it's taken me so long to tell you I love you. For one thing I closed myself off after the divorce, hoarding all my anger and my fears of getting re-involved. You broke through those barriers—but you were so insistent you didn't want commitment that even Caleb's little sermon didn't really convince me you cared for me. I guess I was afraid to admit that I loved you, even to myself, because what was the use? You didn't want me.'

She chuckled. 'Oh no, you've got it the wrong way round—*you* didn't want *me*.'

'We've been a couple of fools, haven't we?' He kissed her at some length. 'Sal, three months ago I told my boss I didn't want to have an affair. For very different reasons I don't want one now. Will you marry me soon?'

She looked down at her jeans. 'Give me five minutes to change.'

He gave an exultant laugh. 'You don't do things by half-measures, do you? It's one of the things I love about you. Do you think we can wait until Saturday?'

'I believe I'm free on Saturday.'

'Good.' He ran his hands down her body. 'Having said that about affairs, it would be a shame to waste an empty house. May not happen again for months.'

'I don't have a double bed,' she murmured.

'Then we'll have to hold each other all the closer,' Luke replied.

Which they did, the whole night through. And when they woke in the morning the sun had already burned off the mist over the cove.

Harlequin Romance

Enter the world of Romance...
Harlequin Romance

Delight in the exotic yet innocent love stories of
Harlequin Romance.

Be whisked away to dazzling international capitals... or
quaint European villages.

Experience the joys of falling in love... for the first
time, the best time!

Six new titles every month for your reading enjoyment.
Available wherever paperbacks are sold.

Rom-1

ATTRACTIVE, SPACE SAVING BOOK RACK

Display your most prized novels on this handsome and sturdy book rack. The hand-rubbed walnut finish will blend into your library decor with quiet elegance, providing a practical organizer for your favorite hard-or soft-covered books.

Only $9.95

Approximately 16" x 8" when assembled

Assembles in seconds.

To order, rush your name, address and zip code, along with a check or money order for $10.70* ($9.95 plus 75¢ postage and handling) payable to *Harlequin Reader Service*:

Harlequin Reader Service
Book Rack Offer
901 Fuhrmann Blvd.
P.O. Box 1396
Buffalo, NY 14269-1396

Offer not available in Canada.

*New York and Iowa residents add appropriate sales tax.